The Nemesis Club

THE NEMESIS CLUB

JENNY SAVAGE

ST. MARTIN'S PRESS
NEW YORK

First published in the U.S. by St. Martin's Press in 1978
Copyright © 1977 by Jenny Savage
All rights reserved. For information, write:
St. Martin's Press, Inc., 175 Fifth Ave.,
New York, N.Y. 10010.
Manufactured in the United States of America

Library of Congress Cataloging in Publication Data

Savage, Jenny.
    The nemesis club.

    I.   Title.
PZ4.S2637Ne   [PR6069.A936]   823'.9'14   78-3991
ISBN 0-312-56379-5

To my friend Jill Butler,
with thanks for her encouragement

PREFACE

To a crime reporter, a murder case quickly becomes a routine job. Nobody wants to read about burglary any more, unless there is a title attached to the victim or the crime has been accompanied by a sufficiency of bloodshed, and so murder and bank robbery, preferably under arms, are all that is left to us. I had imagined it might be an exciting and glamorous job, when I was a starry-eyed schoolgirl that is; vague visions of fast cars, flashlight photography and always a sense of urgency, leaving a lasting impression on my mind. Now all that is gone and perhaps I have drifted too far the other way. All life is theatre anyway, and surely we all act? My speciality is a sort of world-weary cynicism and I often wonder, drifting even further into cynicism, how many people are taken in by it.

After innumerable hours of hanging around police stations in a thick smog of cigarette smoke, butts crushed out in paper coffee mugs, after miles of tramping pavements and talking to the excited, publicity-seeking public, the glamour idea has died; but by the time it had done so my interest had been aroused, and now I would not have it any other way.

If you have ever been to a police station immediately after a major crime, you may have seen us. If we look bored that, at least, is not an act. We are waiting, and probably have been for hours, for somebody to tell us something, often no more than a brief comment, that can be blown up, perhaps exaggerated, and padded into half a column on the front page. Nowadays the police are tolerant of us, and helpful too, especially since they have realised how mass media can help them and enlist public support for their work. In return we have become less demanding. We both have jobs to do, and even from my side I can see why they feel their own work is more urgent.

In the story that I am about to unfold, the reverse was the case. Never before or since had the co-operation of the public been more vital, and we were the link. Any time a major development took place we knew, sometimes within minutes, and there was rarely any need to wait around in a police station. They would telephone us, and a nice change it made, too.

Everybody knows the bare facts of the case now. Everybody was keeping an eye open for the green Vauxhall with the dented front wing, hoping the vicious sadist would be caught soon and, most important of all, keeping an eye on their children.

There is something peculiarly horrible about child murder, and when the killer first rapes, then murders and finally mutilates his victim, the horror is multiplied many times over. There was even more to it than this, but until now many aspects of this strange case have been kept secret.

I became involved entirely by chance. It was decided, politely, that this was not a case for a woman to cover; a decision that left me slightly tight-lipped, but I knew the reasons and had to accept them. Women crime reporters are not so rare now, but even the most hard-bitten policemen can be surprisingly diffident about disclosing the small, very physical, details of a rape case in front of a woman. I had become used to the quick, sidelong glances and the polite euphemisms, but there was no room for them this time.

So I was left in London while the manhunt was on, and

only after a man lay dead in the car park behind a police court did I learn that a chance remark of mine to a young woman photographer had set in motion a chain of events so unexpected, so unheard of, that even the police were shaken, horrified and saddened.

Perhaps it was because of my small, vital part in these events that I decided to tell the story, and my own investigations led me into places unusual even to me. Mainly of course I was in the Midlands, but I spoke to the men in Brighton who knew Eileen Denham, I moved in the circles of her rich friends, I stood in the pale corridors of New Scotland Yard, and I flew the Atlantic on a visit that would barely have justified a telephone call, let alone my wasted air fare. But now I think I know the truth, strange and terrible though it is, and it must be told even if only as a warning. Much of what I say has been pieced together from many different sources, and much I have had to deduce, I hope logically, from what I learnt. But this is what happened.

CHAPTER ONE

The first child died on a Thursday morning in the late spring. Her name was Janice Clayton, and she was twelve years old. Her distraught mother telephoned the police that evening when Janice did not return from school, and a chance encounter with a school friend brought the frightening knowledge that she had not even arrived at school that day.

She had certainly set off for school, smart and bright in the green uniform, a new leather satchel on her back. Two schoolboys remembered seeing her running along the asphalt path through the park on her normal short cut to the red brick building. The man who guided the children across the busy main road outside the school had not seen her. Within the three hundred yards between the playground area of the park and the zebra crossing she had disappeared.

Normally when a child of this age is first reported missing the police are not unduly worried. Nearly always the child returns, unharmed and unable to understand the fuss. Heedlessly, they have been playing with friends, perhaps gone to their home where their parents, less forgivably, have not thought of letting the anxiously waiting mother know. The policewoman who called on Mrs Clayton was comfortably reassuring, speaking of the high rate of truancy, and collecting the names and addresses of Janice's friends.

It was not until Chief Superintendent Alan Black, the head of Hallerton C.I.D., came on duty later that evening that the search started in earnest and he was, perhaps unfairly, angry at the delay but he did have reasons.

Several disturbing incidents, none of them particularly serious in themselves, had caused him to feel increasingly uneasy during the past few weeks. A young girl had been picked up by a man in a car, indecently assaulted in a fairly mild way, and dumped in a deserted lane some three miles away. School children had reported being approached by a strange man in the park who had given them sweets and asked them to meet him again. Young girls had been offered lifts by strangers and the police had issued the usual warnings.

Alan Black ordered an immediate and thorough search of all the parks, the deserted waste grounds near the disused canal, and the common land between Hallerton and Wallington. Resentful policemen were taken to their allocated areas, and the search began. Grumbling, swearing and thoroughly disgruntled, the lines of men moved slowly over the damp grass, beating down the young bracken with sticks, shining their torches into the bushes, kicking aside the grass that overhung the ditches.

At eleven o'clock that night a school blazer with Janice Clayton's name tape stitched inside the collar was found on a grass verge beside the road that ran across the common. Fifty yards further down the road among a clump of bushes, a new school satchel containing school books with her name on the fly leaves hung from a bramble, and the reflection from his torch caught an alert searcher's eye.

When the news of these discoveries was relayed to the other searchers, the grumbling stopped immediately. With a new sense of urgency the search was intensified, the men moved a little more quickly, looked more closely into the entangled bushes, dropped to their knees beside the ditches to scan the muddy water under the matted grass. Tracker dogs were brought up to the common, handsome Alsatians, their tails pluming gaily as they circled through the woods and bounded over banks and hedges.

Men who had hoped to go off duty at midnight shrugged as the clock struck the passing hour, and worked on. More men were brought up from the town, and later those who had completed the searching of the parks joined them on the dark common.

But it was not until the following morning that the pathetic little corpse was found by a mounted policeman, hidden under a heap of bracken alongside a bridle path, far further towards Wallington than the night's searchers had covered.

Sergeant Keith Toller was not supposed to cover that particular path at all. He had come on duty at eight o'clock that morning, and ever since then he had been slowly riding his big bay horse down paths through the woods, scanning the ground to either side for any signs that might lead to a discovery. He was a young man and the horse was fresh and eager; the wide, green path leading down towards the road was a temptation not to be resisted and, with a brief glance over his shoulder to make sure that he was not being watched, he turned the horse towards the path. A harmless break from routine; even if he was spotted, surely a blind eye would be turned to such a minor misdemeanour.

The horse plunged forward, ears pricked and nostrils flared with excitement. Toller steadied him, and then dropped his hands and leaned forward as the fast, even stride developed.

Half-way down the path alongside a steep, tree-shaded bank, the horse shied violently and came to a sudden halt, head thrown up and forelegs braced. Toller was thrown forward half-way out of the saddle, and his face slammed into the upflung neck. He straightened, swearing, his hand held to his

13

painful nose as he picked up the reins again. When he saw blood on his palm he swore again, and reached into his pocket for a handkerchief as he dug his heels into the shaking flanks.

The horse half reared, squealing, spun to one side and then stood trembling, sweat breaking out in dark streaks on his neck and shoulders

Toller stared down in astonishment and then raised his head and looked carefully around to see what had frightened the horse. It was several moments before he noticed the pile of bracken wilting under the overhanging tree, and then he looked at it closely, a frown creasing his brow as he slowly dismounted, looped the reins over his arm, and stooped to look under the dark fronds.

When he straightened up, his face was ashen and he was retching violently.

It was Inspector Dick Farley who told me about the police work that took place after the body was found. He had been Alan Black's assistant at the time, and every relevant piece of information that came back to the Hallerton C.I.D. had at one time or another passed through his hands.

I visited him at his home on the outskirts of Hallerton one winter evening. His wife answered the door, a small, smiling woman, strands of grey lightening her blonde hair, eyes crinkling in welcome. She made us coffee and then went upstairs to play with the children, so our discussion was held against a background of crashes and laughter which suggested their games were somewhat rowdy. Dick Farley occasionally raised his eyes to the ceiling and smiled tolerantly.

He is a tall, grey-haired man, slow moving and slow speaking, considering every question carefully before answering and showing great patience with a lay-woman's ignorance of technical details. I must say in my defence that

I have a reasonable grasp of forensic terminology, but there were times in this case when they became too esoteric for a mere crime reporter, let alone a member of the public.

'We went straight up to the common as soon as we heard she'd been found,' he began. 'Toller was still there, of course, walking the horse further on up the path. He still looked a bit sick, it was the first time he'd seen anything like that. First time any of us had really.'

He frowned, and paused, rubbing his chin thoughtfully. Then he looked at me, leaned forward, and clasped his hands as he sought for the words to explain. 'It isn't so much the sight of the body that shakes you up. You see far worse in road accidents. It's knowing that someone has done this deliberately. Do you know what I mean?'

'Yes, I think so.'

He looked at me closely for a moment, still frowning. Then he nodded, satisfied that I understood, and sat back in his chair again, putting his fingertips together and looking up at the ceiling. 'I don't know if you've seen the pathologist's report. Briefly, she'd been raped and there were injuries from that of course, then her throat had been cut with a serrated edged knife and after that he'd carved up the body just about everywhere. I think when we'd got over our own shock, most of us were thinking about a relative having to identify that. It's always worse with a child, and her face was a mess too. But they did a good job patching her up, and it wasn't too bad in the end. Mrs Clayton's sister came up from London.'

'Just what do you do when you get to the body?'

Farley smiled, and reached for his pipe.

'There are scores of things to do. Most of them are very boring and technical. You have to pack up practically everything for the laboratories, photographs of course, details of

15

wind direction, air temperatures. It's usually hours before you can move the body. Then the whole area has to be searched too, you take plaster casts of footprints, tyre tracks – do you really want all this?'

'Only the important bits.'

He smiled again, and began to tamp the tobacco into the bowl of his pipe, examining it carefully as he spoke. 'It's all important really. But I think I know what you mean. Well, we found tyre tracks further down the bridle path and a man came up from the tyre depot and identified them as Land Rover tracks. We thought they probably were, but we didn't know for sure. So we put out an appeal for the driver to come forward. By the time he did, two days later, we were up to our eyes in it. Hundreds of questionnaire forms were coming in, and we had to go through the lot, quite apart from all the other things. It was Pat Palmer who found the driver in the end. But a lot had happened before then.'

He lit his pipe, speaking between puffs of smoke, his teeth clenched around the stem. Once the tobacco was burning to his satisfaction he relaxed, leaned back, and began to speak more easily, glancing at me occasionally through the smoke as if to make sure that I was still listening.

'I suppose we all dread this kind of thing on our doorsteps. You know, it could be anybody who'd done it. You've got the Press on your back all the time screaming for instant arrests, you put every man you can on to it, you send out warnings, everything you can think of because you know if you don't get him, and quick, he'll do it again. No matter how careful you are. This one was clever, crazy maybe, we'll never know now, but clever. We all knew we weren't getting there fast enough and that was bad. Bad for all of us, and I reckon the Superintendent aged ten years in those two weeks.

'Well anyway, we got everything packed up and taken

16

down to the lab. I remember there were nearly fifty pieces of bracken covering the body alone, and I got a 'phone call that afternoon which nearly blistered my ear drums. When they were searching the wood Hugh Fox found a blood print on a tree, so they carved it out and sent it back to the lab to take prints. Complete hand it was, lovely job.'

'How do you take prints off bloodstains?'

'Leuco-malachite. Do you want me to explain?'

'No!'

He laughed quietly, took the pipe out of his mouth and bent forward as he pressed the smouldering tobacco down into the bowl. 'Okay. Anyway, it turned out it didn't have anything to do with the case, but some reporter found out about it and had a field day. "Caught the Red Hand but Missed the Murderer" was one little gem I remember. And do you know we found nearly two hundred pieces of women's underwear in that wood? Jesus! Hallerton night life! But that hand print didn't cause anything like the trouble we had with the Land Rover.

'Well, as I said, we published an appeal for the driver to come forward. Usually to do them justice they come up, but not this time. Oh, no, not this time.

'So the Superintendent put Pat on to finding him. He went through all the local dealers' records, chased up nearly every Land Rover in the county, so when he finally did get an answer I'm not surprised he was a bit annoyed.'

Farley smiled as he remembered the incident, glanced at my whirring tape recorder, and picked up the box of matches again.

It was three days later that a sheepish young man had arrived at the police station and nervously told the sergeant at the desk that it had been his Land Rover on the common.

The sergeant had telephoned Palmer, who had taken him up to Farley's office and had remained, leaning against the door, as Farley interviewed him. He had merely jerked a thumb over his shoulder as they came into the room.

'Mr Frazer. Drives Land Rovers round the common.'

Farley looked at Palmer warily, and then turned back to Frazer.

'Won't you have a seat?' He gestured towards a chair and leaned back against his desk as the young man sat down gingerly.

'When did you take the car up on the common?'

'Wednesday night.'

'Why?'

'Took my girl friend up there.'

'I see. And when did you take it home?'

'Thursday afternoon.'

Palmer leaned back against the door and looked towards the ceiling.

'The gentleman would appear to be blessed with stamina,' he remarked to no one in particular.

Frazer shot him a look of malevolent dislike. Farley ignored him.

'Would you mind explaining?'

Frazer clasped and unclasped his hands, and stared down at the floor. Farley waited in silence, looking at him questioningly, and Palmer lit a cigarette, stuck it in the corner of his mouth, and narrowed his eyes against the smoke that curled up into them. Frazer glanced at him and drew a deep breath.

'We went up there after the pictures, see?'

'Yes?'

'Well, the battery was flat. So I parked it on the slope, so I could bump start it.'

18

'I see.'

'Well, it rained, didn't it?'

'Did it?'

'Yes. It bloody well did. Anyway, Rene wanted to get home. But it was stuck.'

'What was stuck?' asked Palmer suddenly.

'The car. It wouldn't roll and I couldn't push it. So we had to walk.'

Farley nodded sympathetically. Palmer grinned.

'So I come back with another battery and off we go. I drive it home.'

'How did you get the other battery down to it?'

'Humped it. Didn't want to risk getting the Imp stuck, so I parked it on the road, and carried it down.'

'I see.'

'Well, that's the lot. Okay to go now?'

Farley reached for a notebook.

'All right Mr Frazer, if you'll just give us your address and the name and address of your girl friend, we'll be in touch if we need you again.'

Frazer looked up uneasily. 'What do you want Rene's address for?'

'In a case like this we have to double check everything.'

Later, when Frazer had left, Farley stared sullenly at Palmer and pointed an accusing finger at him.

'You were trying to needle him.'

'Not half as much as he needled me. Three days I've wasted trying to trace that bastard, and why? Because he's scared his girl friend's mother might find out he's been shagging her up on the common. Makes me sick. Can I go home now?'

'Wish you would.'

'Of course,' said Farley, opening his eyes suddenly and

staring at me, 'we were going flat out at that time. House to house enquiries, checking up on anybody with a record of offences against children: you name it, we were doing it. We were getting questionnaires back at the rate of about a thousand a day, or so it seemed when it came to sorting them out.'

'What was the public response like?'

'Great. Dozens of people rang in to say they'd seen the child on that day. Some of them had, too. Not that it really helped much, we'd worked out by then she'd crossed the park all right and she'd been picked up somewhere along Summerville Road. Nobody saw that of course, they never do.

'It wasn't just the general public either. Everybody seemed to buckle down to this one, it was terrific. Take the printers, for example. When we found her we wanted posters up with a photo of her just as fast as we could get them. The printers dropped everything else and did them on the spot. As soon as they were done we needed the questionnaires printed, and they did those right away too.

'Well, it was about then that we got a Clue with a capital C. You probably know you get a lot of cranks attracted by a murder case, especially one like this, and some of them write to the parents. The mother in this case – Mr Clayton had left her years ago and run off to Australia. Some of the letters are really sick, so we always offer to go through the post every morning and check up, you know, filter out the nasty ones. It doesn't take long and it can save a lot of grief.

'It was Julie Saunders who was doing it that day, and she brought back four crank letters and a taped cassette. No markings on the tape, just a spool in a padded envelope, typewritten label on it, posted locally, and thank God she did!

'She went into her office and played it through, and came back to see me, looking as sick as a horse.' Farley fell silent for a moment, his eyes narrowed and lip curled in disgust as he remembered. Then he sat up, and pointed the stem of his pipe at me, jabbing it towards me to emphasise his words.

'That recording had been taken of the whole disgusting thing. It was the most obscene thing I've ever heard, and believe me I've heard some muck. And the mother was supposed to get that!'

I winced and he nodded, his lips compressed. Then he smiled.

'We asked the Press to keep quiet about it while we tried to trace it, and they did. We had what we thought was a real stroke of luck here, because it turned out that the tape was a new experimental sort that had been taken off the market almost immediately, because it faded. They only sold about fifty of them. So the sun seemed to be shining for us.

'Then the luck stopped dead. The cassette was part of a batch that had been stolen from a factory in Essex about six months before and they'd never caught the thieves. They tried again when we told them why, and they tried damned hard too, but they had no luck.' He sighed, and shook his head slowly.

'It was a real stinker. We had nothing to go on, absolutely nothing. All we knew was the killer's blood group from the semen tests, the time of death near enough, where she'd been picked up, and the fact that the man had a cassette recorder. What can you do with that? I don't think we could have done more than we did and, as you know, it wasn't enough. It was just exactly one week later that he did it again. Only one week.'

CHAPTER TWO

It was actually eight days later that Veronica Butler was killed. Her mother owned a hair-dressing salon four hundred yards from the school, and she and her brother Nicholas would walk there together every afternoon when the school closed. Three hundred and fifty yards down the road, round the corner into the busy main shopping street and up the stairs to the salon was surely safe enough, especially in a crowd of children going the same way. Mrs Butler, in common with every mother in the area, had warned her children of the danger, had asked a friend to escort them from school to the door of the shop, and had then felt confident that she had safeguarded them adequately.

This time it was the school that made the unbelievable, unforgivable error. Veronica had complained of a headache, had said she felt sick, and her teacher, having dutifully warned her class of the danger of being in the streets alone, had written a note to Mrs Butler and sent her home, alone, at half past eleven in the morning.

She did not arrive, but it was not until Nicholas came back at a quarter to four that afternoon with the information that Veronica had not met him outside the school that Mrs Butler knew that anything was wrong. She ran back to the school immediately, and found the last teacher on the verge of leaving, with no knowledge of what had happened to Veronica.

Frantically, Mrs Butler telephoned the police. It took the

desk sergeant nearly three minutes to take down the particulars from the incoherent woman, patiently repeating his questions until he finally had enough information to send a patrol car to meet her at the school. A quarter of an hour later they contacted Veronica's teacher, and the hunt was on.

'I've never seen the Superintendent so angry,' said Farley. 'We all thought our problem was with the children, it never occurred to us the teachers needed watching too. We got the road blocks up, teams questioning people in the streets and the houses along the road where she'd been picked up, searchers out on the common again, the whole lot, you know what happens without me telling you. Once we'd got everything started and all we could do was wait for results, the Superintendent hit the roof. He got a circular letter printed the next day, sent it out to all the schools, telling them what had happened and why, and he didn't spare them anything. Of course, when it came to the inquest that teacher was torn apart. She's left the area now I think, don't know where she is. Be understandable if she'd changed her name too, she was a household word at the time. But by then the damage was done.

'We all knew what we were going to find, but you couldn't help hoping. They found her at daybreak the following morning. A frogman in the canal, it was. I was out there then, seemed pointless to hang around listening for the telephone back at home here, so I drove out to see what was going on.

'It was sort of eerie out there. I don't know if you've seen the place, there's a lot of waste ground on one side, warehouses on the other and this great slimy canal in the middle. It doesn't take long to search the ground, but the canal can take a while, and further up there's a bit of woodland too. There was a boat out in the middle, we could hear the voices across the water, but apart from that it was completely quiet. Now and then one of the frogmen would come up and swim up to the boat, then he'd be sent along to another patch and all you'd hear was the water surging as he went down again, and sometimes the oars of the boat and the two men in it talking. There was a car parked on the bank, the radio would start up sometimes, and there were about four of us standing round it waiting for news. I can picture it now, sort of early grey daylight and a bit misty and cold, and the blue lamp the driver forgot to turn off flickering on the water.

'Then one of the frogmen came up alongside the boat and pulled off his mask. We heard him say "she's down there", and one of the men in the boat blew a whistle. A couple of lads who'd been hunting around in the old tip on the other side stopped and looked across the water at us. Then the driver got on the radio while the frogmen swam across and waded out, and still it seemed so quiet and sort of peaceful down there.'

Farley's pipe had gone out, and he sat with it cupped in the palm of his hand, staring unseeingly at the fire, his eyes dark and sad with memories. Then he glanced at me and gave me a quick, apologetic smile.

'As soon as the body was found it was decided to call Scotland Yard in; and there were a lot of people who thought we should have done it sooner. Maybe they were right, I don't know. But we yelled for help right away this time, we couldn't cope with this on our own, not two in a week. Nobody could. They came up that night.

'I expect you know the way the "Murder Squad" works. It's a rota, they take their chance on what it'll be when their turn comes up. What usually happens is you get a senior police officer and his assistant. We got Superintendent Walshe, and right now I'm going to say if Black and I had got together and had our pick, he would have been our choice. He was bloody marvellous. He brought John Stewart with him, and that man never seemed to get tired. We were all just about on our knees at the end of that week, but he just kept breezing along as though he'd just come back from a holiday in the South of France.

'This time it was different. We had the F.B.I. as well. Do you know what led up to that?'

By that time I did know, but many people had been wondering about it and I have heard some fantastic theories put forward. The idea had started some months earlier with a generous gesture on the part of the Federal Bureau of Investigation. One of their scientists had been experimenting in some obscure branch of forensic medicine and had discovered something or other that he considered a major advance in the science. This scientist had obtained permission to pass his findings on to Scotland Yard and he had written to Dr Longhurst, carefully setting out his instructions and employing simple language to ensure that the British police should derive maximum benefit from the advanced techniques used by the F.B.I. without floundering in a mass of technical data they would doubtless find difficult to understand.

With an air of unholy glee Dr Longhurst penned his reply; an abject apology for failing to save the F.B.I. the trouble and expense of research that had been carried out in London two years previously, and a few humble suggestions for methods of use which he ventured to think might be found an improvement.

Unlike the courteous letter he had received, Dr Longhurst's reply was couched in such advanced and obscure technical terms that it became necessary for him to spend two

25

hours in the reference library checking his spelling and usage.

So delighted was he with this incident that for the next two days he became almost affable, and only his assistant was aware of the reason. In the past Dr Longhurst had written three times to his friend in the F.B.I. informing him of improvements and advances he had made, and on only one of these occasions had the F.B.I. admitted they had been unaware of Dr Longhurst's new method.

When his self-satisfaction had abated somewhat, Dr Long-hurst considered the situation carefully. It was becoming obvious that methods used by the F.B.I. and New Scotland Yard were not identical, and both parties might benefit from an exchange of information. At much the same time that Dr Longhurst was discussing plans for an exchange visit with the Commissioner, one Dr Weil of the F.B.I. was swallowing his chagrin and making similar suggestions to his own superiors.

The Commissioner's affably worded invitation for two F.B.I. agents to spend a few months with the Metropolitan Police as active onlookers crossed in the post with a generous offer from the F.B.I. for two senior members of the C.I.D. and two forensic scientists to spend as long as they wished with the F.B.I. studying their methods.

Thus it was that Daniel Hardisty, after three weeks in London, left his colleague poring over microscopes and retorts, and joined Detective Chief Superintendent Walshe and Detective Sergeant Stewart on their long visit to the Midlands.

'What happened when they arrived?' I asked.

'They went down to the police station right away. They knew the body had been found of course, and it's a bit different when it's found in water, because you're unlikely to find anything in the immediate area, so they'd told us to go ahead as normal until they got there. The post mortem was done that afternoon, and the results were much the same as for Janice Clayton.

'This canal's a bit different from most. It isn't still water, you see. It's slow moving certainly, but a body would drift. It had caught on something on the bed of the canal, or it could have been quite a long way further down by then. I think we found her sooner than the killer anticipated. There was a length of chain tied round her legs, heavy enough to keep her under but not enough to keep her in the same place. That was a stupid mistake, because it would obviously catch on something sooner or later, and there she'd stay. Of course, one of the first things we had to do was try and trace that chain. It took a bit of time, but we did it in the end.

'But the first thing they did was go over all the work we'd done up to then. No good trying to do much until they'd done that, and by the time the three of them had got through it all it was getting dark, so there was no point in going up to the canal then, and anyway our own men had been searching the area all day and nothing had been found.

'What they did then was get out a sort of plan of action to try and protect all the children. We'd done quite a lot of that of course, watching parks and playgrounds though they were pretty deserted. We even had three cars taking children home from school in cases where they usually walked and there was no alternative or they couldn't be met. One of them was young Nicky Butler I remember, his mother wouldn't trust anybody else.'

'Boys were in danger too, then?'

He shrugged. 'You never know,' he said thoughtfully, 'and you daren't take chances. But Bill Walshe wanted to take it a lot further than that. He fixed up a system whereby the

27

schools were to ring in with a list of children who hadn't arrived that day and whose parents hadn't telephoned. We got a lot of false alarms of course, mostly when children had been off sick one day and the parents hadn't thought to ring up the next day either, but it didn't take too long to check up usually, except unfortunately in the case of children coming in from the country. But that way he reckoned he could get on the track if a child was picked up within an hour at the outside.'

'You were counting on there being another one?'

He nodded, sighing. 'Yes, we had to. We had no reason to believe he'd stop at two, and plenty of precedents to show he wouldn't.'

'Were you hoping to catch him in the attempt?'

'Heaven forbid! This one had been far too successful to dare bank on that. We made sure all our precautions were well publicised to try and discourage him. Of course, you can sometimes pull off a quick arrest if you get someone on the spot, but that's not much consolation to a dead child or her parents. We wanted to stop it happening again at all costs, even though it meant getting him the slow way. It meant a hell of a lot of work, but by then we had extra men from Wallington to help out.'

Farley chuckled suddenly, and leaned back in his chair, his hands clasped behind his head.

'I remember the Superintendent – Black, that is – ringing up Wallington. Offered Superintendent Doone forty square miles to exercise his police dogs! But they were a great help. We'd never have coped without them.'

'Just how much extra work was there for the uniformed police?'

'Oh, the extra load was enormous. Did I mention question-naires? Yes, I thought so. We'd covered the area round the

28

park where Janice Clayton was picked up, and the probable route up to the common, and the same for Veronica Butler, but Walshe wanted the whole town covered, and a much more exhaustive questionnaire at that. These all had to be taken round and people had to be helped to fill them in. Then in the first four days after Veronica Butler was killed there were two days when we couldn't trace a child, and that meant setting up road blocks and pounding around on that bloody common again. When you reckon there are four main roads out of Hallerton, busy ones at that, and eleven minor ones too, you get some idea of what the road blocks alone mean. Half a dozen men on each main road, at least two and sometimes four on the others, in the morning too when traffic's heavy, then you've got patrol cars haring around hunting for the children or their parents, men searching the same old ground again, and all the time you're collecting information, chasing up every impossible lead, and hunting through all those forms – oh, it was no picnic.'

'Was all this done at the police station?'

'Oh, no, I'm sorry, I thought you knew. John Stewart's main job was setting up an information centre, and we hadn't got room. That was one of those irritating problems that took a bit of solving – finding premises. Nothing seemed to come up until a woman rang in one day and offered us her house – an entire house! Said she had an ulterior motive, and Walshe reckoned it was a speeding offence, but it turned out she was looking after her two grandchildren while their mother was in hospital, and she felt safer with us around. It was a perfect set-up. She owned this big house which she lent to her daughter, the one in hospital, and she lived in a little lodge in the same grounds. The place was likely to be standing empty for a couple of years anyway because it was a T.B. case, so we took all the furniture out and stored it for them and set up home there. Had to do a lot before we could move in, of course, extra telephones to be put in, office furniture, it took us a day and a half to sort it out, but Stewart did all that and by the time he'd got it organised it was working like clockwork. Later on we had fifty people there working round the clock, most of them on filing, but that was when things really hotted up about ten days later. By that time it was all organised, and it was a beautiful job.

'But I'm getting a bit ahead of myself there. A lot had happened before then. The very same morning we discovered the body another tape was delivered. We found it, and it was the same thing, same batch of tapes too, the stolen ones. He'd been quicker this time, it had been posted in the town the afternoon before. Now what Walshe reckoned was that both times we'd found the body sooner than the killer thought we would. The first time he'd probably reckoned on a few days' grace, because it was the first one and, as far as he knew, we might reckon on her having run away or being kidnapped or something, so there was no hurry about posting it. He knew the balloon would go up with the second one, and he nearly made it, too. We found the body at four, and the tape came through Mrs Butler's letter box at eight. We'd have checked her letters anyway, but he wasn't to know that. Walshe said that next time one of two things might happen with those tapes. Either he'd hide the body more carefully, or he'd deliver the tape in person.

'Now, that seemed unlikely to me. I mean, it's a hell of a risk, isn't it? Even if there's nobody there when he calls, there's a fair chance somebody will see him. I never thought he'd have the nerve, though looking back on it why I should have thought he lacked nerve I can't imagine.'

'You thought there would be a next time then?'

Farley nodded soberly. 'Yes, I'm afraid we did. You can't

watch every child every minute of the day and we'd been getting dozens of reports, literally dozens, of children being found in the streets alone. Even after two cases! You'd be amazed how stupid people can get. My two never set foot outside the house, let alone the garden, unless Cathy or I was with them, but people never seem to realise. It was mostly at weekends or after school of course, and it was just impossible to watch everywhere all at once.'

'How did the public take it on the whole?'

'They were marvellous. They all wanted to help. Of course, you get a few stroppy ones, but most of them were as helpful as could be. You come across problems with that, too. Some people "remember" strange men hanging around, that sort of thing, when they haven't seen anything at all. I suppose they think it encourages us or something, but you can waste hundreds of hours if you're not careful, and you daren't pass up anything like that. The one old biddy you write off as a crank may be the one with the sharpest eyes in the street, and maybe she really did see something important.

'Anyway, to get back, we all thought he'd have another go sooner or later, and the most we could hope for was that we'd get on the trail soon enough. After all, it was over two hours between the time Janice Clayton was picked up and the time she died. Probably less with Veronica Butler, but we could only hope.'

'Weren't you getting anywhere at all by this time?'

Farley frowned thoughtfully as he considered the question. 'If you mean, had we any idea at all of who'd done it, then the answer's "no",' he said slowly. Then he glanced at me, and pointed his pipe at me admonishingly. 'But I wouldn't like you to get the idea that all the work we'd done was a waste of time. We had a rough idea of the sort of man we were looking for, or maybe that's putting it too strongly. We were

31

looking for a man who had a car, or the use of one at the particular times, he had a cassette recorder or ditto and, one of the main things, if we could find any tapes from that stolen batch, we were as good as home and dry. By this time we were about resigned to a process of elimination enquiry and it was being done mainly through the questionnaires. We had a lot of important questions to ask on those forms, and the main ones were "Do you own a car?" "Where was it between the times A and B, C and D?" The same on the tape recorder; we asked for blood groups too, although that couldn't be so conclusive because you can't check them all, even the ones who know. We wanted to find out where everybody was at the time, and who could verify it.

'Now, there was one enormous drawback to all this, I expect you've spotted it, and that was we were working on the assumption that the man came from Hallerton. We didn't have any reason for that assumption either, except for the fact that roughly eighty per cent of sex crimes are committed in the home area, but you've got to start somewhere. It left a nasty taste though, starting with a doubtful premise like that.

'There was another thing that helped. You know we'd had a few incidents before the murders? Not many, but more than average and we were beginning to get worried even then. Well, when the big scare started, five women came to the station at different times to tell us their daughters had been accosted by a strange man in a car and two of the girls said the car was green and the man was dark. Now, the girl who'd been assaulted and dumped out in the countryside said the same thing, a green car and the man had curly black hair. That was about all she knew, children aren't very good at descriptions, or if they are adults aren't very good at getting the idea, I sometimes wonder which. This girl said the man was "quite old", but to a nine-year-old that can be anything from twenty upwards. It doesn't sound much, but with the little we'd got we jumped on it. You see, if the girl recognised the man, if we could find anything in that car, anything at all: a hair, a bit of cloth off their clothes, it hardly matters what it is, and link it up with the tapes and the blood group and all the rest, we'd get a conviction. So we really went to town on green cars, we'd no idea of the make at that time. We went through all the tax records, dealers, garages, paint sprayers, and in the end there was hardly a car in the county we hadn't traced.'

'It must have taken a long time.'

'It did take time, but don't forget we weren't working alone at that. At the Motor Tax Department the clerks sometimes worked up to midnight with us going through the records, and nearly all the dealers did the same. They were a terrific help. And of course by the time we were half-way through, we knew the make of the car too.'

'That was after Hilary Denham died?'

'Yes. The third one and, thank God, the last. But of course we didn't know that then. It was the worst one of the lot.'

CHAPTER THREE

Eileen Denham lived with her daughter, Hilary, in a Tudor cottage in a village five miles outside Hallerton. Eileen was a young widow, her husband having died four years previously of a painful and lingering disease of the blood. Robin Denham had left her comfortably off rather than wealthy; she could afford to run her husband's old sports car, a Jaguar XK 120, which she loved dearly, provide Hilary with a pony and keep the lovely little house, but this meant taking a part time job in Wallington during the school term. A woman came in from the village twice a week during the term times to help with the housework.

Eileen Denham had been particularly careful of Hilary's safety when the first warnings had been issued by the police. She had arranged with her friend, Mary Hunter, to take turns to drive both Hilary and Jennifer Hunter to the school and to collect them in the afternoon. Both children had been warned, emphatically and repeatedly, of the appalling danger that threatened them. Both had listened solemnly and then whispered excitedly to each other, thrilled at the situation that caused their parents so much anxiety.

On the morning that Hilary died Eileen Denham had an appointment with her solicitor in Wallington. It was Mary Hunter's turn to take the children to school and, as time passed, she became worried and tried to telephone. The number was engaged.

Five minutes later when she saw Mrs Priddy, her household help, walking up the path, she kissed Hilary goodbye, repeated her admonition not to leave the house until Mrs Hunter arrived, and ran out to her car.

Mrs Priddy was a sour, middle-aged woman, continually complaining of her painful feet and skimping her work as much as she dared. When she arrived that morning she discovered there was no furniture polish left, and asked Hilary to go to the shop to buy a new tin. Hilary protested, and said that her mother had told her not to leave the house. Mrs Priddy at first argued, then whined, and finally lost her temper, shouted at the girl and ordered her to run down to the village at once and stop being insolent. Hilary shouted back that she would tell her mother, then seized her satchel and flung out of the house, slamming the door behind her. Mrs Priddy yelled something at her retreating back, then picked up the basket of washing on the kitchen table and limped out into the garden to hang it on the line. She did not hear the telephone ringing.

Two miles away, Peter Hunter finally replaced the telephone and called up the stairs to his wife.

'Mary?'

'What?'

'There's no reply from Eileen. Shall I ring the doctor now and try again later?'

'Yes, you'd better do that, tell him I think it's measles. You've rung the school, haven't you?'

'Yes, about ten minutes ago.'

Hilary slouched sullenly down the road, kicking at stones and swinging her satchel, resentful and angry. She glanced round as a car swung out from the lane behind her and slowed up as it drew alongside her. The driver leaned across and wound the window down.

'Hello. Going to school?'

Hilary looked at him suspiciously and walked on.

'No, I'm going to the shop.'

The car moved alongside her again.

'School holiday, is it?'

'I'm going to school later.'

'I'll give you a lift.'

'No thanks, I'm going with Mrs Hunter.'

'Okay, I'll take you to Mrs Hunter.'

'She's coming to collect me, and I'm not supposed to talk to strangers.'

'Very wise too, but I'm not a stranger, so it's all right. I'm Mrs Hunter's brother, and she asked me to look out for you. She's hurt her arm, you see. Come on, jump in.'

The door swung open. Hilary stopped and looked at the driver uncertainly. He jerked his head impatiently.

'Oh, do come on! I haven't got all day you know.'

'Why didn't Mrs Hunter telephone?'

'Because she was sending me, of course. Look, love, hurry up will you? I'm late already.'

Reluctantly, Hilary climbed into the car, and pulled the door shut. She was still gazing worriedly at the driver as the car pulled away and roared down the road.

Back at Hallerton police station a thoughtful doctor on his early morning rounds called in with a warning that a measles epidemic was likely. Walshe sighed wearily at the news, and began to consider ways of dealing with the inevitable difficulties that would arise as a result. He was not surprised when the desk sergeant rang to say that five children had failed to arrive at school without notification. Yet again the road blocks

36

were set up, the necessary information was radioed to the patrol cars and the men were taken up to the common.

Had Hilary Denham lived in Hallerton her life might have been saved by this prompt action. As it was, the implications of her particular situation were not realised until the names and addresses of the missing children were brought up to the C.I.D. offices nearly twenty minutes later, and by then it was too late. Cursing himself wildly for not foreseeing this eventuality, Walshe ordered cars to be sent out to Little Kirkton and an immediate search to be made for the one child still unaccounted for.

By the time the patrol car called at the Denhams' home, Mrs Priddy, having skimped briefly through her work, had left a terse note, 'No furniture polish so have gone home. E.P.', and had done just that. The people in the houses on either side were away, and the woman in the cottage further down the road had no knowledge of Hilary's whereabouts, or of how to contact Mrs Denham. The driver radioed the news back to the police station, and drove on into the village.

Some time later, when the new road blocks were being set up, a young patrolman glanced admiringly at the dark green Jaguar that roared past him, automatically wrote down the registration number, and stepped into the road, holding up his hand to halt the next car. Eileen, glancing briefly in her mirror, saw him write in his notebook, looked uncertainly at her speedometer, and shrugged as she drove on.

On the other side of the village a young man in a green Vauxhall noticed a police car speeding towards Little Kirkton, and frowned. They'd been quick this time.

Eileen pulled up in front of the cottage, reaching into her handbag for the front door key, and walked into the house, humming quietly to herself. She dropped her handbag on to the small table in the hall, and turned to close the door. As

37

she did so, she saw the cassette lying on the doormat. She picked it up in surprise, turning it over in her hands, puzzled. Then she laid it down beside her handbag, and walked into the drawing-room on her right.

Mary Hunter lit a cigarette with shaking hands, and looked worriedly at the policeman standing in the doorway.

'My husband tried to telephone Mrs Denham, but there was no reply,' she said. 'Jennifer's got measles, you see, and I couldn't leave her. I thought Eileen was probably bringing Hilary here, then I assumed she'd taken her into school herself. Oh, good heavens, what can have happened to her?'

'Do you know where Mrs Denham is now?'

'Yes, she has a job in Wallington, she'll be there. Just a moment, I'll get the address for you.'

Black laid down the telephone and turned to Walshe.

'We just haven't got enough men to cover all this,' he said. 'Wallington are sending us thirty more and they're covering the moors for us, but there's a lot of woodland around Little Kirkton. Shall I take some off the common?'

Walshe drummed his fingers on the desk and chewed his lip.

'No, don't do that. Anything come in from the road blocks?'

'Not yet, nobody's seen anything, and there's a big traffic jam building up.'

'Yes, there will be.' Walshe spoke slowly, his eyes dark with worry. 'I'm afraid we're too late for that. Take them down and put the men on to searching those woods.'

'There still won't be enough,' warned Black.

'I know, but we can't use more men than we've got. Has anybody found Mrs Denham yet?'

38

'No, she took the day off work. Had an appointment somewhere.'

The driver of the patrol car walked back down the road and stepped off the kerb, holding up his hand. The grey Rover obediently slowed and pulled up beside him. He walked round the car and bent down to speak to the man at the wheel.

'Sorry to bother you sir, we're looking for a missing child, dark haired girl about ten years old, probably in a grey school uniform. Have you seen her?'

'No. No, I haven't. This isn't another one, is it?'

'Hope not sir, thank you all the same.'

'Good morning madam, sorry to bother you, we're looking for a missing schoolgirl, dark haired, ten years old, grey school uniform. Have you seen anybody like that?'

'No, I'm sorry. Is this the same thing again?'

'We hope not. Thank you madam.'

'Officer?'

'Yes madam?'

'Good luck.'

'Thank you.'

The co-driver of the car leaned out of the window.

'Jack? Radio call. We've got to stop here and go up to the woods by the church.'

'Okay.'

Eileen muttered irritably when she found Mrs Priddy's note half an hour later, and noticed the undusted furniture. Then she ran upstairs to change.

On the way down, she caught sight of the cassette lying on the hall table, picked it up and tossed it up in her hand, eyebrows raised in query, then carried it through into the drawing-room. She took out her small recorder, fiddled with it for a moment, snapped the tape into place, laid the recorder down on the table, and walked towards the kitchen.

She had reached the door before a faint click announced the beginning of the recording.

Walshe methodically ticked off the last of the items on his list and looked up as the tall American walked into his office.

'Finished?' he asked.

'All done through there. What's to do now?'

'Could you go down to the school and get a photograph of her? Send that back with the driver and then talk to her friends, see if they know anything. Do you know the sort of thing?'

'Sure.' Hardisty turned back to the door.

'Oh, Dan!' Walshe looked up and smiled. 'I haven't had a chance to say before, but we do appreciate your help.'

'You're welcome.'

In the village, Sergeant Fox took the small walkie-talkie set out of his breast pocket, pressed a switch and spoke into it briefly. After a moment the radio crackled with an answer, and he pressed the switch again.

'A Mrs Clements of Riderswell Cottage says she saw Mrs Denham drive away at about 8.45 this morning, but she was alone. Headed for the main road towards Wallington, green Jaguar XK 120, number unknown. She also says Mrs Denham's daily should have been there today, but she didn't see her. A Mrs Priddy, lives at one of the cottages by the church.'

The radio buzzed for a moment, and then a voice came through.

'Get all the details from Mrs Clements. Inspector Farley will go and see Mrs Priddy.'

Mrs Clements smiled at him. 'Come on in, I was just going to make a cup of tea.'

As Fox removed his hat a helicopter swung out from over the trees, hovered briefly, and turned back towards the woods again. Mrs Clements stared up, her eyes narrowed against the sun.

'That's the second time I've seen that! Isn't it low? I wonder what they're doing.'

Fox squinted up into the sun.

'Same as us, I think.'

'Oh? Well, I do hope you find her. Poor little thing.'

In the town, the dust from the road was spiralling in little eddies behind the cars and lorries. The few pedestrians were dressed in summer clothes, and were moving slowly along the pavements. It was too hot for hurrying.

The drowsy hum of the traffic was shattered by the demanding blare of an angry horn, and the big green Jaguar hurtled recklessly through the crawling vehicles, the engine howling in low gear. Brakes squealed and voices rose in angry protest, but even the crunch of a collision and the crash of breaking glass did not slow the car, and the tyres shrieked as Eileen hurled it through the corner against the red light, forcing pedestrians and traffic alike to crowd hastily aside for the skidding Jaguar.

Eileen screeched to a halt in front of the police station, stalled the engine, leapt out and, without even a glance at the scratched paintwork and dented panels, bounded up the steps and burst through the door.

Hardisty flicked open his notebook and handed it to Walshe.

'No special friends except Jennifer Hunter. None of the children know anything, but her teacher was quite sure Mrs Denham would have telephoned. If anything suspicious had happened Hilary would have told her mother, and so far as they know she hasn't said anything.'

Walshe shrugged. 'Thanks anyway.'

'Ah, look, for Pete's sake stop thanking me, will you?'

'Okay. I'm afraid this is going to be a long, slow job.'

'I'd noticed. You'll know from the films how different it is in the States. We'd have been shooting it out with him by now.'

Walshe's chuckle was interrupted by the shrill demand of the telephone. He picked it up, and spoke his name.

Hardisty watched the smile fade from his face and his mouth whiten as the desk sergeant spoke. He acknowledged the call briefly, and hung up.

'Mrs Denham's on her way up. She came home and found a tape recording – and she's played it.'

CHAPTER FOUR

'By the time I came in she'd been there about half an hour,' said Farley. 'Things were a bit quieter by then, but Walshe said it had been pretty good hell up to that time. Of course, she was shaky and a bit incoherent, but she seemed to have got herself under control.

'I think when she'd heard that tape her one idea was to get it to the police as quickly as she could. Well, she did that okay, it took weeks to sort out the damage she caused on the way, but until she got there she hadn't really given herself time to think. It wasn't until she put that tape on Walshe's desk that she could forget about that and think about what it meant, and you can imagine what happened.

'Well, that was a painful time – a very personal experience – I don't think too much ought to be said about it. You may not agree with me, but if you don't you're going to have to get your information somewhere else.

'After I'd seen that old cow Mrs Priddy I came back to the station and went up to see Walshe. Mrs Denham was still there and Dan Hardisty was asking her questions while I told Walshe what had happened. Dan was very good at that sort of thing. He got a lot of answers quickly, but he wasn't unsympathetic or anything. I don't know what it was, some sort of attitude he had, he could ask anything. If I'd asked Mrs Denham some of those things she'd have gone up the wall in screaming hysterics, but she kept her self-control with him.'

43

'What sort of questions would be so difficult to ask?'

'I'm sorry?'

'I mean, what did you need to know from her that would have set her off? Wasn't it mostly what time she'd left and when she'd got back, and those sort of things?'

'Oh, I see. Well, yes, all that came into it of course, but we had to know more than that. It isn't so much the questions, it's the implications behind them, why we need the answers. And in the state she was in anything might have happened.

'It didn't take very long to get her evidence in the end. We got a statement written out and she signed it, and then we had the problem about what to do with her. You can't just say "Thank you very much, Mrs Denham, we'll be in touch" and show her out of the door. She hadn't any relatives around, and her only close friend was Mrs Hunter, who was tied up with her daughter having measles. Really she should have gone into hospital, but she put her foot down over that. She wanted to go home, and she started to get upset when we argued, so we said we'd take her home and call her doctor. I think he got a nurse to come in and stay with her.

'Then she started getting jumpy about her car, she'd got to the stage where she was picking on details and worrying about them. We said we'd bring her car along later, but she wouldn't have that, she wanted to go home in her car, she didn't want a W.P.C. to go with her and she started to cry again.

'Then Dan offered to drive her home in the Jaguar and stay with her until she got a doctor, and she grabbed that idea. It was a bit irregular, but it didn't matter much, and we had a lot to do and we just wanted her out of the way by then. We had an awful lot of search parties to organise, and we'd hardly even started.'

*　　*　　*

44

Hardisty drove the car cautiously, careful to avoid the slightest incident that might startle his passenger or make her nervous. He had sat in the car for a couple of minutes, familiarising himself with the strange controls, sliding the seat back to accommodate his long legs, adjusting the mirror. Eileen had leaned back in her seat and closed her eyes, opening them briefly as Hardisty started the engine, and then turning her head away to stare out of the window.

They drove in silence until the houses thinned out and the cars were fewer. Then Eileen brushed the hair out of her eyes and looked at the man beside her. She smiled tiredly.

'This is kind of you.'

He shook his head, and glanced down at her.

'It must have seemed silly,' she continued apologetically, 'wanting to go home, and wanting the car.'

'Not to me.'

'Won't you have a lot to do?'

'I don't have to do anything. I'm only over here courtesy of Scotland Yard.'

'Why?'

'It's an exchange visit. Seeing how you work over here, we may find something we can use in the States.'

'Is it very different?'

'Not really. It seemed like it at first, but I guess it was more a difference in size than anything else. You get used to thinking in thousands of square miles, and then it comes down to tens. Like working in miniature. In the sort of things I was doing, anyway.'

'I don't think I understand that.'

'Well, take search parties for example. In the States any outlying areas would be covered by helicopters, and they'd have maybe two hundred square miles to go over. Or you'd ask for three hundred men to search a forest. Now it's ten

45

men to go through some little wood here, thirty to cover a park, that sort of thing.'

'Have you found anything that might help back in America?'

'Not me. Not yet, anyway. I've got a friend working in the laboratories in London. He's come up with one or two ideas.'

Eileen sat up and pointed.

'That lane there. About two hundred yards down on the right. The house with the white gates.'

The little boy hung head downwards from the tree and stared curiously at the naked girl on the bank, his face innocently curious in the way of young children. As the blood ran to his head and began pounding uncomfortably he pulled himself up into the tree and looked back down the path at the woman walking towards him.

'Mummy, there's a girl here with no clothes on,' he called. 'I think she's hurt.'

'Oh, do stop shouting Tim.'

'She's all bloody. Maybe she's dead.'

'What did you say?'

'I said "Maybe she's dead".'

The woman reached the tree and smiled up at him.

'Who, darling?'

He pointed down at the other side of the bank.

'Her.'

'People behave in funny ways when they find a body,' said Farley. 'You can never tell how anybody will react, even quite sensible, intelligent people. Especially in a case like this. Sometimes they'll hang around it for hours, not doing anything, just staying there. Sometimes they'll telephone the police, anonymously, then just disappear. Something about a dead body seems to fascinate some of them: they touch it, handle it, run away, come back again, look at it again, run off again, sometimes you'd think they'd gone completely off their heads.

'The woman who found Hilary Denham, Mrs Graham. Perfectly ordinary sort of woman, sensible, level-headed type, you'd never have imagined the sort of havoc she could cause, all with the best possible intentions, too. She sent her little boy back to the telephone box on the road to call us, a perfectly sensible thing to do really. Then she thought the man might still be around, so she called out to him to bring him back. He didn't hear, so she was going to run after him, then she thought she couldn't leave the body in case somebody else came along, so she wanted to cover it up. She hadn't got a coat or anything, so she started to scrape up earth and piled it on top of the body. Completely crazy. By the time she came to her senses that bank looked as if a bulldozer had been over it. Then she realised what she'd done and ran off down the path to find her little boy.

'Well, he'd found a policeman before he got to the telephone, and she met them both coming back along the path. Told him what she'd done, couldn't apologise enough, and he radioed in and told us what had happened.

'Poor woman. It wasn't her fault really. But you'd never believe how people can behave in that situation.'

Eileen stared distractedly round the room, and started nervously as Hardisty closed the door behind him.

'Would you like a drink?' she asked.

He smiled down at her. 'Why don't you just sit down and take it easy?'

'I'd much rather be doing something.'

47

He looked at her consideringly for a moment, and then nodded and smiled again.

'Okay. But if it's not too much trouble I'd prefer a coffee.'

'It's no trouble.' She turned towards the kitchen.

'Say, can I use your telephone?'

'What? Oh. Yes, of course. It's on the table by the fireplace. Why do you need it?'

He moved over to the table. 'I promised I'd call your doctor. I'll make trouble for myself if I don't.'

'Oh, I see. It's Doctor Siddons, the number's in the book.' Eileen smiled shakily, and went into the kitchen.

When she came back a few minutes later he was standing at the window looking out over the lawn towards the paddock where the grey pony grazed under the trees. He turned as she came in.

'He'll be right over,' he said.

'Oh. Good. Why don't you sit down?'

It was at that moment that the telephone rang. Eileen jumped, stared at it, and then looked back at Hardisty, her face whitening.

'I'll get it.' He strode quickly across the room and lifted the receiver.

'Hello? Yes, speaking.'

He turned his back on her and listened for a few moments. Then he hung up, and turned round.

Eileen was standing just behind him, looking mutely up into his face. He put his hands on her shoulders, and spoke quietly.

'They found her. They were too late. She's dead.'

For a moment she stood rigidly, staring up at him. Then her eyes closed, and a great, shuddering sigh broke from her, and she crumpled forward against him.

48

Her last memory before a merciful unconsciousness took her away was of his arms holding her against him, and his voice speaking gently in her ear.

'I don't really think there's very much more I can tell you that would help,' said Farley. 'It was only a couple of days after that that Superintendent Black asked me to take over the day to day stuff to leave him free for this lot. Walshe is in Germany at the moment, isn't he? Yes, I thought so. Maybe you'd better try and see John Stewart.'

'He's on leave.'

'Oh. Well, what do you want to know about next?'

'I'd like to find out a bit more about Dan Hardisty.'

Farley nodded slowly, and thought for a moment. Then he smiled.

'I think you'd better go and see Pat Palmer.'

CHAPTER FIVE

Pat Palmer lives in a small bachelor flat in the centre of Hallerton. He and Dick Farley are good friends, but two more different characters would be difficult to imagine. Where Farley is cautious and reserved, Palmer is flamboyantly self-confident. He is strikingly good-looking, tall and tanned, with bold bright eyes and an Irish brogue that is surprisingly attractive when he remembers to use it. However, the slightly flashy first impression is a clever cover for a quick, intelligent mind and a dogged determination that had been rewarded by rapid promotion once he had joined the C.I.D.

He poured drinks for us both, settled me comfortably in an armchair, checked my tape recorder for me, flung himself into a fireside chair and looked at me expectantly.

'Fire away, sweetheart. What do you want to know?'

'What was your position in this case?'

'As now, Detective Sergeant Patrick Palmer, totally at your service.'

'Thank you. What did you do?'

'You want to know *everything*?'

'All the important bits.'

'Ah. Now that fines it down a bit. What important things did I do now? John Stewart was setting up his little incident room, or information centre, or whatever it was he chose to call it. Dick Farley was temporary boss, and loving every minute of it. The Superintendent wasn't too fit just then, so that left me, you see.'

'To do what?'

'Somebody had to be messenger boy to the big white chief. Run all his errands and stir his coffee. It isn't everybody who appreciates my talents in this field, obvious though they may be. So I got every dead end job there was, starting with a certain Land Rover...'

'Yes, I heard about that.'

'You did? If it was from Dick Farley it was probably a biased and libellous account, but we'll let that pass and I promise I'll not sue you. When everybody started doing some work, an unusual situation that nearly frightened the life out of them, I was told to tell them what to do. That's what's known as "passing the buck", or taking grave risks in the furtherance of your duty. So. When it came to checking up on cars, I had to fix that up in the tax offices, ask the clerks to help. Setting thieves to catch a murderer, but perhaps I shouldn't have said that. Lovely people, all of them, damn their eyes, but they did work. Oh yes, they worked very hard. Didn't help one little bit, but they did their best.

'And setting up search parties, but that only happened twice when I was on the spot, praise God. Working out how many men we'd got and who I could send where without getting shot for my trouble.'

'Did they object?'

'They didn't dare, poor cowed devils. You've no idea of the tyranny that goes on in the Police Force, darling. It'd make your heart bleed.'

'What else did you do?'

'There's not a bit of mercy in the woman. Is that not enough? It seemed like it at the time.

'But, since you ask, I did a lot more. The whole thing was run on those question and answer forms. No doubt Dick will have told you, grabbing all the limelight for himself again. Now, if we got an answer on one of those forms that needed a second look, about once every million questions that would be, I had to go out and take that second look. Or if there were a lot of second looks to be taken I had to fix up some other poor devil to do it too. That's what I mean by dead ends.'

'I see.'

'Now you've come to a dead end yourself, haven't you? That line of questioning's got you nowhere, and me neither, so have another drink and we'll both try again.'

'No, thank you. Can you tell me something about Dan Hardisty?'

Palmer groaned, and covered his face with his hands.

'Isn't that the story of my life?' he demanded. 'Every woman I meet wants to know about Dan Hardisty. What's he got that I haven't? And I'm much more available.'

'Well, he played a rather bigger part in the story.'

'Now that's unfair. Given a chance I'd have played a big part too, had my picture all over the papers and all the pretty girls feeling sorry for me.

'However. You want to know about Dan Hardisty, so I'll forget my broken heart and try to help you. What do you want to know about him?'

'Let's start at the beginning. What did he look like?'

'Yes, all good stories start with that, don't they? So. What did he look like, now? Height, about six foot six, never gave us poor midgets a chance.'

He looked at me quickly to make sure I'd caught the point, and grinned.

'Comparatively speaking, that is,' he conceded. 'Weight, about twelve to thirteen stone, build, thin. No doubt you'll describe him as "lean" to make him a proper hero. Hair colour brown, eyes brown, distinguishing marks scars on face and hands.'

'Even then?'

'Ah, no. That was later, wasn't it? I'm sorry. Distinguishing marks, none. Will that do?'

'Very good. But I still don't know what he looks like.'

'Ah, darling, have a heart! I can't give you a woman's magazine description!'

'Thank you very much. I'm not writing for a woman's magazine.'

'Sweetheart, I'm contrite. What can I do to make up for it? Switch that tape recorder off and have another drink to show me I'm forgiven.'

'You're forgiven. I'll just write him up as tall, dark and handsome, shall I?'

'It would be a lie. Tall, yes, dark, perhaps but handsome, never. Why, his face looked as if it had been carved by a drunken lumberjack in the pitch dark with a blunt axe. He was not handsome. Would you believe me if I said he had buck teeth and a squint?'

'No.'

'I thought maybe you wouldn't. Ah, well. Could you not just look at some photographs of him and let me off this hook?'

'Yes, all right.'

'Ah, but I've a better idea now. Come down to the nick tomorrow, and I'll do you an identikit picture of him.'

'I think I can manage on photographs thank you. Tell me a bit about his character.'

'His character now. Where will it end? I can't help you with his childhood, so don't ask. His character. Well, he was quiet. It took a while to get to know him. Very efficient, mind you, oh yes. If you set him to do a job, that job would be done. But he wasn't a talkative man at all.

'He had a sense of humour mind, I'll say that for the dirty

53

bastard. You never found out about it 'til weeks later when it turned out the last laugh was on you and he'd known it all the time and never said anything about it.'

'Can you give me an example of that?'

'I could give you dozens. He rented this flat in Hallerton you'll remember. Real luxury. He never did that on the miserable pittance they give a copper, not even in America. You know what his explanation was?' The Irish brogue switched to an exaggerated nasal drawl. ' "Grand-pappy struck oil." Did you ever hear such rubbish? Struck oil! Now, it has often occurred to me that there must be some basis of truth in this idea about American oil millionaires, or the cliché would never have started.

'At least,' he amended, 'it's occurred to me now. We none of us believed him, of course, and he just laughed and wouldn't say any more. So we all looked very foolish when it turned out that was just exactly how he had got his money. And then he added insult to injury by saying his grandfather had been digging a hole in the ground to put up a "For Sale" notice, and a big black gush of oil had come up and blown him clear back into his senses.

'Well, you never know, stranger things have happened, and we'd made fools enough of ourselves the first time, so we believed him and let it go. And then we found out his grandfather had been a famous oil prospector and never done a bit of digging in his life with anything smaller than a drilling rig.'

I laughed. 'Didn't you like him?'

'Oh, yes, I liked him well enough. I worked with him for a long time, and we got along fine. He was nice enough, friendly when you got to know him. We'd often go out for a drink together, we had many a good laugh.'

'Did you never have any idea of what was going on?'

'Now, what would you be meaning by that? He would never talk much about Eileen Denham if that's what you mean, so I never knew what she was planning. I knew he was crazy in love with her, but that was quite a while later, and even then he'd never say much.'

'He took her home when Hilary was killed, didn't he? Did it start then?'

'Ah, no. No, I wouldn't think so. He stayed with her most of that day, but that was just common humanity. He waited until the doctor came, and then stayed until the nurse arrived. You wouldn't have him go off and just leave the girl, would you?

'For myself, from my own ideas about all this, I don't think any of this would have happened, any of it at all, if she hadn't come back into Hallerton later on that week, on the Saturday it was, and met him again then. I think it was after that she got the whole idea.'

Eileen had gone into Hallerton because she had received a vicious letter from a man who claimed to have killed her daughter. For three days the police had checked her post, but nothing unpleasant had been found, and so she had told them not to bother. Reluctantly, they had agreed, and on the Saturday morning a letter had arrived so gruesome and horrible in its lascivious detail that she had felt sick when she read it. She had overcome her first impulse, which was to burn it, and had taken it into Hallerton as she had been asked.

When Hardisty had arrived at the police station that morning Walshe had suggested that he take the day off and have a well earned rest. It would be the first day he had not been working full time since they had arrived in the Midlands and so, on Walshe's assurance that there was nothing important for him to do, he had agreed.

He was half-way across the reception area before he saw Eileen standing at the counter, and as he stopped and looked at her she turned towards him. At first she looked at him blankly when he smiled at her, but then she recognised him and smiled in reply.

'Hallo,' he said, walking back towards her. 'What are you being booked for?'

'Oh, I got a letter. I brought it, somebody saying he killed Hilary, you see, I thought I'd better...'

'Oh.' He interrupted her, grimacing slightly. 'One of those.'

'Yes.'

'Don't get upset about it. People write them, they're a bit sick, they don't know what they're doing.'

'Yes. Yes, I see.'

He offered her a cigarette, lit it and leaned back against the counter as a constable came through the connecting door and spoke to Eileen.

'If you'll leave the letter with us Mrs Denham, we'll deal with it. I'm sorry you've been bothered like that.'

She smiled at him vaguely, and turned back to Hardisty.

'I'm sorry, I'm a bit dopey this morning,' she apologised. 'Are you going out? Can I give you a lift anywhere?'

He held the door open for her, and stepped out into the sunlight, looking up into the clear sky.

'Would you like a drink?' he asked. 'I've got the day off.'

'Are the pubs open?' She looked down the road at the Jaguar parked by the kerb. 'Yes, I suppose they will be,' she went on, not waiting for his reply. 'I'd like a drink. Thank you.'

They walked to the car in silence, and she stood beside it, hesitating.

'I'm so sorry,' she said at last, smiling apologetically. 'I'm

56

so vague at the moment. Would you mind driving?'

'Sure.'

He took the keys from her, and held the door open.

'You've got the day off?' she said as he started the car. 'That's nice. Would you like to borrow the car? I mean, you haven't got one, have you?'

'That's very kind of you.'

'Oh no. You were kind to me. I shouldn't be driving, I get muddled and do silly things, and people shout at me and then...' She ended with a sob, and Hardisty glanced at her in concern as she fumbled in her handbag for a handkerchief.

'Oh, I'm so sorry,' she whispered. 'It's so silly, but I can't help it.'

He reached into his pocket.

'Here.' He handed her a large white handkerchief, and she took it gratefully.

'Thank you. I'm sorry.'

'It's all right. Look, would you like to come out for the day? We could get out for a drive in the country, the fresh air might do us both a bit of good.'

'Oh, no, I couldn't. You take the car, and enjoy yourself.'

'Please. I'd like your company. If you're not doing anything else.'

She shook her head. 'No, nothing else. Thank you, I'd love to.'

'That's great. We'll go back to my place first, if you don't mind, so I can get changed out of my city slicker suit.'

Hardisty's flat was in a small mews not far from the police station. It overlooked a narrow cobblestone yard where the old stables had been converted into garages and the lofts above them into small self-contained flats.

Eileen looked around vaguely as they reached the top of the stairs.

'This is nice,' she said politely.

'It suits me. Can I get you a drink?'

She shook her head, and he smiled.

'Still full of drugs?' he asked.

'Oh, no. Not that. I can't take them, you see. They make me ill, so the doctor says I can't have sedatives and things.'

'That's bad luck. Well, sit down and make yourself at home. There's some magazines there, I won't be a minute.'

He walked through into the bedroom, and Eileen wandered around the room looking at the pictures. She stopped in front of a photograph on the mantelpiece. It showed a young boy in jeans and a T-shirt holding a small hunting rifle and triumphantly brandishing a dead rabbit. The boy's face was alight with happiness and pride, his eyes narrowed with excitement.

She picked it up as Hardisty came back into the room. He had changed into slacks and was pulling on a heavy sweater.

'Who's this?' she asked.

He glanced at the photograph. 'Terry. My son.'

'Oh. Yes, I can see, he looks a bit like you. I didn't know you were married.'

'I haven't been for the last two years.'

He had opened the lid of a desk in the corner of the room and was searching through a pile of letters. He looked up as Eileen walked over and leaned against the wall beside him.

'Do you see anything of Terry?'

'Oh, sure. When I'm home he spends his vacations with me.'

Eileen glanced down into the desk, and then stared as the gleam of metal caught her eye.

'What's that?'

He followed the direction of her glance. 'Oh. That's a gun.'

'May I see?' She held out her hand.

He looked at her in surprise, and then handed her the gun. She held it gingerly, turning it over in her hands, the heavy metal awkward and unfamiliar.

'It's yours, is it? I've never seen one like that before. Isn't it heavy? Funny, I always thought they'd be much lighter than that.'

Hardisty smiled, and she caught his glance and handed the gun back to him.

'I'm talking nonsense, I'm so sorry. Here.'

He slid the gun into the drawer of the desk.

'Are they powerful, those things?' she asked. 'I mean, I don't know, I've only seen them on films and things.'

He looked at her musingly.

'Well,' he said slowly, 'if it doesn't actually blast your head off it'll take a fair sized chunk out of it.'

She stared at him blankly for a moment, and then began to laugh, genuine amusement shining out of her eyes.

'What a *horrible* way of putting it!'

He grinned down at her. 'It was your question, lady. Are you ready to go? Come on then.'

As they turned towards the door the angry, monotonous wail of a siren sounded at the end of the road. It grew louder as the car turned into the mews, and then shut off abruptly just outside the door.

'Oh, no!' Hardisty looked ruefully at Eileen.

'Oh dear. That'll be for you, won't it? Is that the end of your day off?'

'Could be.'

The doorbell shrilled.

'Wait here, I'll see what gives.'

She sat down on a low studio couch as Hardisty ran down the stairs. She heard him open the door.

'Sorry to bother you, sir.' The voice was low pitched and

unfamiliar to her. 'A man's been seen dragging a little girl into a car. I was told to collect you.'

Eileen stiffened, her eyes narrowing and her fingers unconsciously curling into claws.

'Okay.' Hardisty's voice was matter of fact. 'Eileen?'

'Yes?' she called back mechanically.

'I'll ring you here if I'm going to be more than half an hour. That okay?'

'Fine.' Her voice was casual and uninterested.

She heard the door slam and footsteps fading. A moment later an engine roared into life, and the siren started again. The car turned quickly on the cobbled stones, and the sound gradually diminished.

She looked down, and saw with detached surprise that her clenched fists were white at the knuckles. Slowly, tears welled out of her eyes and ran down her cheeks.

'Oh, God,' she whispered. 'Oh, dear God.'

As the car speeded down the road Hardisty leaned back in his seat and turned towards the driver.

'What happened?'

'A woman rang up about five minutes ago. Her daughter saw a man dragging a child into a car.'

'Where was this?'

'South Street. Outside the cinema.'

Hardisty stared at him. 'Hell, there must be dozens of people who saw it!'

'You'd think so, wouldn't you? He's got a nerve!'

'I suppose it wasn't a green car?'

'No. A white Cortina.'

'That's all we need. How many cars has he got, for God's sake?'

'Maybe someone got the number this time.'

'Yeah, and maybe pigs will fly.'

Back at the flat Eileen stood up and walked quickly over to the corner cupboard. She poured herself a large whisky and drank it fast, choking slightly as she did so, and put down the glass, hearing it clatter on the table. She clenched her fists to stop her hands shaking, and paced over to the window, staring down into the mews.

From far away, the sound of a siren met her ears.

Another one started up, closer this time.

She closed her eyes and drew a deep breath, her head thrown back as the tears began to roll down her cheeks again.

The sirens faded into the distance.

Angrily, Eileen brushed the tears from her eyes and turned away from the window.

Down in the mews, a child called out.

Eileen started, whirled back to the window and looked down as a little girl with long black hair ran across the road, laughing. She gasped, and threw up the window.

'*Hilary!*'

The child turned and looked up in surprise.

Eileen stared down at the strange face. Numbly, she closed the window and turned away.

Just outside the mews, another siren started.

Eileen clapped her hands over her ears, her teeth clenched on her lip.

'*God damn him!*'

Her scream echoed mockingly round the empty room.

'*I'll kill him! I'll kill him!*'

Blindly, she ran to the desk, wrenched open the drawer and seized the gun. She stumbled down the stairs, opened the door, and slammed it shut behind her.

The little girl stared in astonishment as the green Jaguar

screamed away from the kerb and tore out into the main road.

Hardisty's pessimism had been misplaced. Someone had indeed taken the number of the white Cortina, and within minutes it was radioed through to all the cars.

Fifteen minutes later a prowling patrol car spotted the Cortina parked in a road on the outskirts of Hallerton. The engine was still warm. A few enquiries at the houses elicited the information that the car belonged to a Mr Dobson. One of the neighbours pointed out his house.

He came to the door in answer to the bell, and looked enquiringly at the officers standing at the door.

'Good morning?'

'Good morning sir. Do you own that white Cortina parked across the road there?'

'Yes?'

'I wonder if we might have a word with you. Can we come in?'

'Certainly.'

It did not take long to clear up the misunderstanding. Mr Dobson had taken his small daughter shopping, and she had looked at the stills displayed outside the cinema and demanded to be taken to see the picture. When her father had refused she had thrown a tantrum. He had angrily pushed her into the car and driven straight home.

He called the little girl downstairs, and she had tearfully told the officers the same story. Mr Dobson had been faintly amused, and had congratulated them on finding him so fast. With apologies for having bothered him, they left, and radioed the information back to the police station.

The patrol car dropped Hardisty at the entrance to the mews, and then drove on. Hardisty raised his eyebrows in surprise when he saw that the Jaguar had gone, and then shrugged with faint regret and walked towards the door.

As soon as he entered the flat he saw the ransacked desk, and his eyes narrowed as he strode across the room and checked the empty drawer. Swearing softly, he pulled open another drawer, and took out a heavy box of cartridges. When he saw the seal was unbroken he fell silent and frowned in puzzlement. After a moment he replaced the box, slammed the drawer shut angrily, turned and ran back down the stairs.

Eileen sat in the Jaguar with the canvas hood rolled back. Her shaking hands were clasped around the butt of the heavy automatic, holding it between her knees. She looked closely into every police car that passed her, and some of the drivers glanced at her curiously, but none of them stopped. All the men in them wore uniforms.

She started violently as a shadow fell across her, and her head spun round.

Hardisty stared down at her, his face cold with anger. 'Give me that gun.'

She looked at him in silence, making no move. At last she drew a deep breath.

'Where is he?' she whispered.

He did not reply. For a moment he stood still, watching her closely.

'You're not going to shoot anybody. Give it to me.'

'No.'

His hand flashed down and seized her elbow. She gasped, and tried to wrench free, but he caught her wrist and twisted it hard. The gun slipped from her fingers, and he caught it before it hit the floor. He let her go, and straightened up, sliding the gun into his pocket.

She stared at him wildly as he turned away, and then

bowed her head against her arms on the steering wheel, and began to sob convulsively.

Hardisty looked back at her uncertainly. For a while he stood gazing down at her, and then he sighed, and bent down.

'Move over.'

She looked up, her face streaked with tears.

'What?'

'Move over. I'll drive.'

Obediently, she slid across into the passenger seat as he opened the door.

'What are you going to do?'

He pulled the door shut behind him, and looked at her bleakly.

'Right now, I don't know. We'll go back to my place and talk about it.'

He leaned forward and pressed the starter.

They drove back to the flat in silence, and when they arrived Hardisty put the gun back in the drawer, locked it, and put the key in his pocket. Eileen, sitting on the studio couch, looked up quickly as the key turned, and then her head dropped and she stared down at her hands, clasped in her lap.

Hardisty took cigarettes and a lighter from his pocket and tossed them on to the couch beside her.

'Here.'

She jumped at his voice, and looked at the cigarette packet. She opened it, took one, and tried to light it, but her hands were shaking so much that she could not work the lighter, and after a moment Hardisty crossed the room, took it from her and flicked it into flame. He stood looking down at her.

At last he spoke. 'What did you imagine you were going to do with an unloaded gun?'

She looked up in quick surprise. 'Unloaded?'

'Sure. You didn't think I'd leave it lying around loaded, did you?'

Eileen stared at him blankly. Then she shook her head slowly and ran her fingers through her hair distractedly.

'I don't know,' she said. 'I didn't think of that.'

Hardisty frowned thoughtfully, and then sighed.

'Oh, God. You're in shock again, aren't you? Come on, I'd better get you to a doctor.' He bent down and took her arm.

'I don't want a doctor.'

'Look, honey, you're not well, you need...'

'No, please!'

She jumped up and tore her arm free, her eyes wide with fear. She began to shake uncontrollably, and the tears started to her eyes again.

He stepped forward quickly and put his arms around her shoulders, holding her close to him and stroking her hair soothingly.

'All right. It doesn't matter, it's all over now.'

'There was a little girl, you see,' she said incoherently. 'I thought it was Hilary, and the sirens all over the place, I heard that man say there'd been another one, I just couldn't stand it, I couldn't stand any more, I just took the gun and I wanted...'

'I know. It doesn't matter. Maybe I'd feel the same way.'

She threw her head back and stared up at him, her hair streaked across her face.

'I couldn't stand it any more, you see, I couldn't...'

He smiled down at her and pulled her head back against his chest. 'It's okay, I understand.'

Eileen leaned against him gratefully, her face buried in the rough wool of his sweater, her hands clutching his shoulders. Gradually she stopped shaking and began to breathe evenly again.

65

He stroked the hair away from her forehead as she looked up, a slight, concerned smile on his lips.

'Okay now?'

She nodded, and smiled shakily, brushing the tears from her eyes with the back of her hand.

He bent his head and kissed her lightly on the forehead, and his arm tightened around her shoulders before he turned away.

'Let's get out of here,' he said. 'We could both do with some fresh air.'

'Dan?'

He looked back at her questioningly. She was watching him anxiously.

'What are you going to do?' she asked. 'About the gun, I mean?'

He smiled reassuringly.

'What I should have done right at the start,' he said lightly. 'Put it in a safer place.'

'Didn't he tell anybody about it?' I asked as Palmer finished speaking.

'He never said anything to me about it, sweetheart, if that's what you mean, but it came out later that he'd asked Walshe what he should do. Now normally they might have cut up a bit rough, but Dan had locked the gun away in a steel gun cabinet by then, and anyway nobody could have known what it might lead up to. We had enough on our plates, because we found a man who'd seen the car with the little girl in it, and he did us a bit better than just the colour. A very observant man, was Mr Treanor.'

66

CHAPTER SIX

Andrew Treanor had been working in his garden on the morning Hilary Denham had died. His house was on the road on the other side of the village, very near the woods where her body had been found.

Unfortunately for the police, he had left the house at noon' that day, and gone to London to spend a few days with his married daughter. Naturally, he had heard the news of the murder, but had not realised that he might have vital evidence to contribute until he returned, when he saw posters which mentioned that the murderer had in all probability used a green car. It was then that he remembered having noticed such a car, and he had immediately telephoned the police.

Pat Palmer had driven out to see him, and had questioned him closely.

'Why was it that you noticed this particular car?'

'Well, there's a very dangerous bend just a few yards down the road, you see. There's been a couple of nasty accidents there. I heard this car coming, and it sounded as if it was going a bit fast, so I looked up, and sure enough it skidded right across the road there.'

Palmer nodded, and leaned forward.

'Did you notice who was in the car?'

'I saw a little girl. That was really why I remembered, you see. It was a child's life he was risking, so I was a bit annoyed.'

'You didn't notice the driver?'

'No. He was on the other side, so I couldn't have seen him so well anyway.'

'But it was a man?'

Treanor thought carefully for a moment, and then smiled.

'You know, looking back on it, I'm not even sure I can swear to that. Maybe I've only just come to that conclusion.'

There was a long silence while Palmer considered his next question. Then he looked across at the old man hopefully.

'Can you remember just what it was you thought when you saw that car skid and the little girl in it?'

'Well, vaguely. It was something on the lines of "crazy young thug". Something like that anyway.'

'Crazy *young thug*?'

Treanor sat up suddenly. 'Yes. Yes, it was! I *knew* it was a man, and I *knew* he was young!'

'Just a minute, Mr Treanor.' Palmer smiled. 'Now, a lot of people, if they see a car being driven too fast, they automatically assume there was a young man at the wheel. Do you not think you might have done that?'

Treanor shook his head emphatically.

'If you'd ever driven with my wife you'd never make that assumption again. No, funnily enough I don't like young people generally, but I'm not prejudiced against their driving. If I said "crazy young thug" you can be sure as dammit there was a young man driving that car.'

'Well, that's fine Mr Treanor. That's a great help. Now, I suppose you didn't by any chance notice the make of the car?'

'I did!' The old man slapped his hands on his knees triumphantly. 'I *did* then. My brother had a car just like it. Vauxhall Viva it was, and I'll swear to it anywhere you like.'

Palmer grinned.

68

'You just may have to do that,' he said. 'This is grand! I wish every witness was as observant as you.'

'Yes.' Treanor chuckled. 'Good eyes, I've got, and my memory's not going yet.'

'Did you catch the number?'

'No. No, I didn't.' His face fell ludicrously, and then he became indignant. 'Damn it, young man, I can't go writing down the number of every...'

'It's all right, I was joking. Now, can you remember anything else about this car? You know, was it clean or dirty, rusty, did it sound as if the engine was in good condition, anything like that?'

Treanor pursed his lips and put his head on one side.

'I don't think so,' he said eventually. 'It wasn't there very long. I don't think it was exactly new, you know. Not sort of clean and shining, but I couldn't really be sure.'

'Was it very noisy?'

'No-o. No, I don't think so. But then again, I couldn't be sure of that.'

'Never mind. Do you remember about what time you saw the car?'

'Well, I can't be exact about this, mind. But I went out into the garden at about half past eight I should think, and I hadn't been working there very long.'

'About half an hour?'

'Not as much as that, I don't think. Maybe, but I wouldn't think so.'

'What did you do when you learnt all this?' I asked.

'It cut down the work in one way. No more sniffing around every Rolls-Royce in the country. But in another way it wasn't so funny. Well, we know the answers now, but when we'd checked every green Viva in Hallerton and still not found anything it was a bit of a bugger. If you'll excuse the expression. They all blamed me, of course. They always do when one of their budding Sexton Blake ideas doesn't come up.'

'Why you?'

'I'd been told to check all the cars, you see. Not personally, mind, but it was my job at the time. So they all got on my neck. Then they decided they'd have a go at the Wallington records, and they gave me that job too. Sheer spite, that was.'

'And after that?'

'Well, what about after that? He never taxed the bloody thing anyway, did he? Crafty dodger. So no wonder I couldn't find anything about it, according to the tax office the car had been scrapped nearly a year before.'

'You didn't think of checking up on scrapped cars?'

'No, and I didn't think about looking for the killer in an old ladies' home either.'

'Sorry.'

'Ah, you're forgiven. For the sake of your bonny blue eyes. If they'd been brown, I'd have broken all your teeth.'

'So, not being able to get anywhere with the car, what else did you do?'

'You've no heart at all. I didn't do anything else. At that time, you may remember, we didn't know it wasn't going to get us anywhere, and Vauxhalls are very common cars. It took a long time.'

'Well, apart from you, what else was being done?'

'Ah. Well, there was a grand little scheme afoot at the time, thought out by Beelzebub himself I shouldn't wonder. But there you are.

'What it was all about, you see, was these attempted abductions. You know, there'd been some girls come forward

70

and told us about it. A load of old rubbish we got too, sometimes. Teenagers wanting their names in the papers. But none of the little girls seemed to know the make of the car for sure. As for the driver, all we really knew from them was that he was dark.

'Girls aren't much good at identifying cars usually, and he never tried to pick up a boy. But one of the girls said a man in a green car had offered her a lift outside the park, and a whole lot of boys had seen it, so we tried to trace them. Found four of them, and, would you believe it, none of them could identify the car either!'

'So much for your dig at ignorant girls.'

'Yes, all right, they're all brilliant. But maybe just a little unobservant, if you'll forgive me.

'So then there was this bright idea to teach them how to identify cars. Advertised it we did, we poor suckers, a big teach-in at Hallerton nick, with about three hundred Dinky toys for models.

'Forty of them arrived, damned little limbs of Satan, and very orderly they were. Oh yes. For about three bloody minutes. Then they nearly tore the place apart. Bored stiff, they were, and not one born teacher on the whole force. They all had Dinky toys better than ours for one thing, and one of them got hold of a radio, and knew how to work it what's more, and reported a bank robbery. Bloody mayhem.

'Well, finally we cleared them all out and sorted out all the damage they'd done, and we weren't going to try that again, not for any reason under the sun.

'But the Superintendent wasn't going to let go of the idea. Why should he? He didn't have to clear up the mess. He wanted the brats educated and that was that.

'Then Davies came up with another idea, may he be forgiven. Instead of showing them toys, why not show them

71

films? Get on to the film companies and ask for any old cut out bits that showed cars. Preferably bits packed with a lot of action and even more blood.

'The Super loved that idea, and so did the film companies. Lots of free publicity. So they sent along a van-load of old bits and pieces, and most of it was useless. You can't show ten-year-olds rape scenes, their mothers would lynch you, and from what I heard that accounted for about seventy per cent of the stuff, and then practically every decent bit of film with a good shot of a car used Jaguars. Film men think it's the only car thieves use.

'Well, they don't. They use Fords. More of them, not so easy to spot. But Vauxhalls? Not one in the whole batch. I reckon that company could sue them for unfair discrimination.

'Then Davies had another idea. Proper little brain-wave factory, he is. We'd make up a bit of film of our own, but just a bit different.

'You remember that time when the little girl was nearly picked up outside the park? And there'd been kids in the park at the time, but they'd not been much help?

'Now, Davies's idea was to make a film of that incident, but there'd just be a flash of a car, not enough to say for sure what it was. Maybe it'd jog a memory somewhere.

'Bloody daft, I said it was, and I still think so. Just not reasonable, no matter how you look at it.

'In fact, it's that daft I still get shivers up and down my spine when I think of the result. Uncanny, it was.'

The film show had been cleverly arranged. Before it started, every child was given a pencil and a piece of paper, and told to write down everything they could remember about the car in each sequence. Farley had shown stills of various cars, including a Viva and, apart from the one vital sequence, each car showed up clearly in the film.

All went as planned. When the lights came on every few minutes, the children wrote busily, policewomen helping the younger ones with their answers.

When the short film of the Viva was shown, it seemed at first as if the idea had failed. All the four boys who had been known to have been in the park were, like the other children, grumbling mutinously, complaining that it was unfair. Even the little girl who had been involved sat staring blankly at the screen.

Luckily, Farley spotted Ian Talbot before Davies switched off the lights again; a small, sandy haired boy, sitting at the end of the second row, frowning with concentration and scribbling furiously on the sheet of paper on his lap.

Ignoring the growing murmurs of discontent among the children, Davies waited until Ian had finished writing, and had sat back in his chair, looking expectantly at the screen, before he switched off the lights.

When the show was over, Farley and Walshe examined Ian's paper.

From the point of view of the police, it was perfect. There were no errors and, when the boy had not recognised a car, the paper had been left blank.

There was a detailed description of the green Viva, which bore little resemblance to the car that had been used to make the film, apart from colour and make. Ian mentioned a dented front wing, rusted sills and damaged hub caps.

The Talbots lived in a small, semi-detached house in one of the residential areas of Hallerton. When Farley knocked on the front door it was opened almost immediately by a small girl who bore a striking resemblance to Ian; obviously a younger sister.

73

'Good morning, madam,' said Farley gravely. 'Is your mother at home?'

A dark-haired woman in a blue overall came out of a room at the end of the hall and hurried forward, putting the child to one side.

'Sorry. I was just putting a pie in the oven. What can I do for you?'

'Mrs Talbot? We're from the police. Your lad Ian came to our film show this morning, and it looks as though he may be able to help us.'

Mrs Talbot stood aside. 'Come in. I'm afraid he's out just now, but he won't be long.'

They stepped past her into the hall.

'Don't let us hold you up,' said Walshe. 'If you're working in the kitchen, can't we join you there?'

'It's in an awful mess,' she said doubtfully.

'Should see the state of mine!'

She laughed. 'Come on then, I'll make a pot of tea.'

The kitchen, though tiny and cluttered, was bright and spotlessly clean. Walshe glanced around approvingly as he sat down. Mrs Talbot set out cups and saucers and filled the kettle at the sink.

'Now, how can Ian help you?' she asked. 'You're on this murder thing, aren't you?'

'Yes, that's right.' Walshe hesitated. 'Well, we tried a little experiment on the children this morning. We made a film of our own based on an actual incident. It was like this...'

Mrs Talbot listened carefully to Walshe's explanation as she made the tea. When he had finished she poured it out, and sat down in silence. She stirred her tea thoughtfully.

'That's very odd, isn't it?'

'If it was any lad but Ian I'd have chucked it out as being pure imagination,' said Farley.

74

She smiled at him. 'He's a bright lad,' she said with quiet pride. 'I don't know where he gets it from, because I was the death of my teachers and his father's no genius for all he's a smashing hard worker.'

'Have you any idea how he might have got that description?' asked Walshe.

'He often goes to the rec. after school, so I suppose he might have seen something. Funny he didn't tell me.'

'He probably didn't know what was going on.'

There was the sound of the front door slamming and running footsteps thumping down the hall. The kitchen door burst open and Ian hurtled into the kitchen. He stopped short as he recognised Farley, and turned to his mother.

'What you done?' he demanded.

They all laughed, and Mrs Talbot cuffed him affectionately.

'Sit down here and I'll tell you.'

The stool creaked protestingly as the boy landed on it.

'Remember that film of the Vauxhall Viva?' asked Farley. Ian nodded.

'Would you know that car again?'

'I dunno. Lots of Vauxhalls around. Did I win?'

'Don't know yet, we haven't checked.'

'What's the prize?'

'Pipe down, will you? You haven't won yet. If we showed you a picture of a Vauxhall, could you draw the marks in on it?'

Ian looked at him enquiringly.

'Why?'

'Never mind why. Could you do it?'

'Can I see the film again?'

'No.'

'Can't really remember it now. Might be able to if I could see the film.'

'Try and remember that film.'

Ian stared at him. 'What's so important about that car?'

'Nothing.'

'Oh, come off it, sir!'

'Don't be cheeky, Ian,' snapped Mrs Talbot.

'Sorry, Mum.' The response was automatic.

Farley and Walshe looked at each other. Walshe shrugged faintly.

'It's like this, Ian,' said Farley. 'You couldn't have seen all the details you wrote down from that film.'

Ian looked blank.

'The film was a trick. A little girl was nearly kidnapped just like that by a man in a green car about five weeks ago. That's what you must have seen.'

Ian's mouth fell open. 'Ooo-er!'

'We've got to find that car. And so far you're the only one who's been able to describe it in any detail. Do you often go to the rec.?'

'Most days after school.'

'Can you remember that car?'

Ian cupped his chin in his hands and frowned. 'I think so,' he said doubtfully.

Walshe turned to Mrs Talbot. 'Can we borrow the lad for the rest of the day?'

'He hasn't had his dinner yet.'

'We'll get him a meal in the canteen.'

Mrs Talbot looked at Ian. He was looking unhappy and worried. He glanced at her briefly, his lips compressed. She put down her cup and turned to Walshe.

'Now look,' she said, 'don't get me wrong, I'm as anxious as anybody to see you catch that man. But Ian's only nine, and you're asking a lot of him. I'm not having him worried, and if you try to get him into court I'll have him out of the country. So just remember that,' she finished defiantly.

Walshe and Farley exchanged startled glances.

'I don't think there's any question of Ian being called into court,' said Walshe carefully. 'He hasn't even witnessed a misdemeanour, let alone a crime. All he has done is see the car that was very probably used by the man who murdered Hilary Denham.'

He took out a packet of cigarettes and offered them to Mrs Talbot, who took one and held it between her fingers as she listened.

Walshe reached for his lighter and flicked it into life.

'Now,' he said, 'we've got to find that car. We could just broadcast a description. Green Vauxhall Viva, damaged near-side front wing, and all that, but it wouldn't have anything like the results of showing a picture. Ian's name wouldn't be mentioned, obviously, and we'd make it clear that the marks weren't exact. It would make a tremendous difference. If he can't do it, we'll bring him home and forget it.'

Mrs Talbot looked at Ian, and reached across the table and took his hand.

'It's up to you, love,' she said. 'If you don't want to do it, don't worry. But if you think you can, you ought to try. Suppose it was little Tina next time?'

Ian nodded, his face serious. He looked at Walshe and swallowed.

'I'll try, sir.'

Farley put a hand on his shoulder. 'Good lad. Don't you worry, you'll do fine.'

'He tried very hard,' said Palmer reflectively. 'They gave him outline drawings of Vivas and a bundle of coloured pencils, but he couldn't get the hang of it, and the more he tried the worse it got.

'Just when they were about to give up, Dan Hardisty walked in. He's got a boy of about the same age as Ian, so they told him what was going on and he helped a bit, but it wasn't much good.

'Then Dick Farley suggested we get hold of a scrapped Viva, and make the marks on a real car. Ian said he thought he might manage better on that, so off we all went to find one.

'There's a dealer just outside Hallerton called Bill Woodcock. Right rogue, he is, sell his grandmother for sixpence and flog you a dud car without blinking. But he's got a passion for kids, dotes on them. His place is always swarming with them.

'When we told him what we wanted and why, he couldn't do enough. Found an old Viva, hammered it back into shape, sprayed it dark green, and towed it round with an old Land Rover. Didn't want anything for all the work he'd done except five minutes with this bastard when we found him, and no witnesses. Plenty of people wanted that!

'Well, anyway, there was the car. Now all it wanted was marking up, and that was an afternoon I'll never forget. We brought the lad round again, and there was Dan and myself and Dick Farley, capering around with cans of rust-coloured paint and club hammers and screwdrivers, wrecking this poor old car. Then John Stewart turned up, along with the photographer, and said if that picture was going out on the television he wanted twice as many men as before in the incident room, or they'd never manage. He was right, too.'

'But you didn't get anywhere?' I asked.

'Oh, in the end we did, if you remember. Might never have caught him if it hadn't been for Ian Talbot's description. Though I admit at the time it didn't seem to have worked.

'Come to think of it, I'm not so sure about that either. If we hadn't got that picture out, and if it hadn't been so accurate, he might have tried again. Must have jolted him a bit.'

'What was Eileen Denham doing all this time?'

'The last time I saw Eileen Denham right up to a few months ago was at her daughter's funeral. Mrs Butler and Mrs Clayton went along too and they were standing at the gate of the churchyard talking when it was all over.

'We know now they all went back to Eileen Denham's house later, and that was where the whole idea got thrashed out. But at that time we had no idea. Who could have imagined what they planned out between them? Even now, it still seems too fantastic to be true.'

CHAPTER SEVEN

Contacting Diane Clayton, who had changed her name again, was no easy task, and when I finally ran her to earth in a small flat in Brighton she flatly refused to see me. So I wrote to her, explaining what I wanted and a few days later she telephoned me. Her attitude was not exactly gracious.

'Yes, you can come, but I'll tell you exactly what I bloody well want to and not a word more. Christ, I remember you – you'd crucify your own mother if you thought there was a story in it.'

She had changed considerably since I had last seen her. Her hair was greying now, there were fine lines around the clear eyes and a jerky, nervous manner of speech that was entirely new to me.

She made us coffee, more from force of habit than from any desire to be hospitable, and then sat down and looked at me warily.

'All right. What do you want?'

'What I'm trying to do is find out how three normal, intelligent women got themselves into the fantastic situation of planning the murder of a man they'd never seen.'

'Pretty simple, isn't it? We had a good enough motive, God knows.'

'Revenge? Only about one murder in untold hundreds is committed for that. One of you, maybe, but three?'

She sat in silence for a few moments. Then she looked up curiously. 'What does Anne Butler say?'

'She refused to see me.'

Diane smiled wryly. 'More sense than me, obviously,' she commented bitterly. 'But if one of us doesn't tell you about it God knows what sort of vitriol you'll write.'

I decided it was wiser not to answer that and there was a long silence.

'I was a bit surprised myself when Anne agreed to help,' she said at last. 'She thought we were mad at first, couldn't believe her ears. Not that she did much really. Murder by omission – she didn't stop us. I don't think she ever really believed Eileen would go as far as she did. But it was different for her anyway.'

'How?'

'She still had a child. Nicky. Eileen and me? We had nothing. And Anne was a different type – more sort of placid and philosophical.'

'And you're not?'

She shook her head vehemently. 'I couldn't accept that that was all there was to it. That Janice was dead and I was to do nothing more about it. Nothing at all.'

'Had you some idea of revenge before you saw Eileen then?'

'Idea? No. No idea. But I'd dreamed about it. Lived on it. Never knew I could hate so much.'

'But it was Eileen who made the plan?'

'Some bloody plan that was. Get a gun and shoot him, that was her plan. Never held a gun in her life before. Apart from that burst of idiot hysterics. No. We thrashed that out later.'

'You and Anne and Eileen?'

She shook her head again. 'Not Anne. All Anne agreed to do was stay in Hallerton and tell us the moment anything happened. She said she wouldn't stop us. That's all. She had that much hate.'

'It was all based on nothing but hate?'

81

'Oh, hell!' She leaned forward and clasped her head in her hands. 'Yes. That's all. We spouted a lot of stuff about the desirability of a death penalty and all that, but it didn't mean anything much. We just wanted the bastard dead.'

I waited until she had straightened up and looked at me again.

'Why did you go to Hilary's funeral?' I asked.

She shrugged. 'Seemed the right thing to do at the time.'

'Wasn't it a bit odd?'

'I didn't think so. Neither did Anne. She went too, remember.'

'And you talked to Eileen at the gate of the churchyard?'

'She asked us back to her house. We went.'

'Why?'

'Oh, don't be so stupid! How could we refuse?'

'I see.'

'I doubt it!'

'Look, calm down, will you? I'm just trying to get the picture.'

She didn't answer, and after a moment I went on. 'How did she broach the subject?'

'She didn't. Anne did.'

'*Anne?*'

'Yes. I can't remember exactly what was said, but we were talking about what the police were doing. Anne said something about it all seeming a bit pointless, because the children were dead and he'd spend the rest of his life in a comfortable jail, and Eileen said "not necessarily" and that was how it started.'

'What was said then? Just tell me as much as you can remember.'

Diane frowned and stared at the window. 'I knew exactly what she was getting at right then,' she said at last. 'Funny

82

really, because Anne said "No, you're right. Fifteen years maybe" and I couldn't think what she meant at first. So Eileen put it a bit more plainly, and Anne jumped up and said she was mad, it was fantastic, same old string of clichés. You know the sort of thing.'

'Don't you like Anne?'

She shook her head. 'Not much. Got no time for door-mats.'

'What happened then?'

'Eileen told her it wouldn't do any harm to listen. And I suppose I didn't look particularly outraged. She blustered a bit and then she sat down again.'

'Eileen must have been very convincing,' I commented.

She looked at me quickly, her eyes narrowed. Then she leaned forward and spoke slowly and emphatically. 'Look, you. While you're writing this thing, remember one thing, will you? Just one thing. We didn't *need* much convincing.'

She stared at me for a while, and then sat back and reached for a cigarette.

'She was clever, Eileen,' she said. 'She saw right away she wasn't going to get much help from Anne, so she said "I don't want you to do much. Just let me know if anything happens, like if he does it again and they start tearing around in police cars and helicopters. I'll do the rest."'

'Did Anne agree to that?'

'She didn't really believe it. I think she was a bit scared. She just sat there for a while. And Eileen said "I bet you don't pray for me to fail." Anne just wanted to get out. She said okay, she'd telephone Eileen if anything happened, but she didn't want to know anything else about it. Then she got up and walked out. I didn't think we'd ever hear anything from her again. Except that she might have told the police about us.'

'What would you have done if she had?'

'Denied it. Said we were discussing a hypothetical case, she got the wrong idea and stormed out before we could explain. No problem. They'd have thought she was daft anyway, coming out with a story like that.'

'And in the end she did telephone Eileen.'

'Yes.'

'Why?'

'How the hell should I know? Ask her.'

'Okay. What happened after she'd gone?'

'I told Eileen I'd help her.'

'Tell me something,' I said. 'It came out in court that at that time Eileen had never used a gun in her life, but you had, and you were quite a good shot. Why was it Eileen was to do the shooting, and not you?'

'That was the way she wanted it.'

'And you just accepted that?'

'She had more reason.'

I looked up in surprise. 'I'm sorry, I don't understand that.'

'No. I was surprised they didn't make more of that in court. They just passed over Eileen's background as though it didn't matter at all. I thought it was the most important aspect of the whole thing.'

'Do you know about her background?'

'As much as anybody, I suppose.'

'Will you tell me?'

She bit her lip, and looked at me uncertainly. I leaned forward.

'Look, Diane,' I said, 'I'm not writing for a newspaper now. I'd like this to be an unbiased account, and I'm not putting in any sort of moral comments of my own. If you won't help me on your side of the story, I can't get the

84

full picture, and it won't be as unbiased as I'd like.'

She hesitated, and then nodded.

'All right. But I'm not a writer, I'm a photographer, you'll have to try and imagine what it all meant to her.'

'I'll try.'

For the first time she smiled.

'Eileen was born in 1944,' she began. 'Out in Singapore. Her mother was Eurasian. Half Siamese half Irish, I think, but I'm not sure of that, and she married a Scottish civil engineer in Singapore a couple of years before the war. I don't know why, but when Singapore was invaded they couldn't get her out. Her husband was killed during the invasion, and she was left stranded.

'After the war her husband's father, MacNeil his name was, went out to Singapore to try and find out what had happened to his son. He found out he'd been killed in the shelling and no one knew what had happened to his wife. It took him a long time, but at last he traced her. Well, not her exactly, because she had died when Eileen was born, but he found Eileen.'

'Eileen was born in 1944?' I interrupted.

'That's right. Her father was probably a Japanese soldier. For obvious reasons, they didn't try to trace him.'

'Good God!'

'As you say. Well, Mr MacNeil took Eileen back to Scotland with him, and he and his wife brought her up in Glasgow.'

'Just a minute,' I said. 'How did he find her? And how had she survived after her mother died? And how did he get her out of Singapore?'

Diane gestured impatiently. 'I don't know. But he did it anyway.'

'Okay, never mind.'

'Well, they didn't have a lot of money, but they did their best for Eileen. You'll have seen photographs of her. She was absolutely lovely. Very effective combination, that. Oriental, with those big dark blue eyes.'

She laughed. 'Sorry. That's what you get for talking to a photographer.'

'Oh, don't worry. I quite agree.'

'Where was I? Oh, yes. Well, the old people died when she was about seventeen, I think.'

'Both of them?'

'I'm not sure. Now you come to mention it, I think Mrs MacNeil died a couple of years earlier. But when she was seventeen they were both dead anyway. They left her with a little money, but not very much, so she got a job as a hostess in a night club in Glasgow.'

'Couldn't she have done better than that?'

Diane's mouth twisted wryly. 'The way she'd been brought up the job that paid the most money was the best job. If a docker was paid more than a doctor, then Christiaan Barnard would have been a mug to be a doctor.'

'As bad as that?'

'Maybe not. But anyway Eileen wasn't particularly gifted, except with looks, so she used that.'

'Was she a prostitute?'

'No, I shouldn't think so. I doubt if Robin Denham would have married a prostitute.'

'When did he come into the picture?'

'Pretty soon after that. He met her in the night club. I think he was in Glasgow on a business trip. He was about twenty years older than her you know.'

'Yes?'

'Well, he was fairly well off. Something to do with banking, I think. As I said, Eileen was very lovely, probably lonely,

86

and she certainly had at least half an eye to the main chance. I think she married Robin Denham almost entirely for his money and he was probably infatuated with her.'

'Doesn't sound very promising.'

'No, but it worked out. He bought the house in Little Kirkton, taught her a lot, gave her everything she wanted. But I don't think that mattered to her after a while. She absolutely adored him. Even four years later when she talked about him you could see it. It wouldn't have mattered if he'd been a tramp in the end.'

'When was Hilary born?'

'About a year after they were married. She was absolutely, supremely happy.'

'What went wrong?'

'He died. He got some sort of cancer of the blood and it wasn't an easy way to go. He was at home at the end, with a couple of nurses living in, and Eileen was with him all the time. Drugs weren't having much effect. It must have been hellish.'

'Yes. What happened after that?'

'Eileen had a nervous breakdown. I knew she'd been ill, but I didn't know it was mental, I promise I didn't know that!'

'All right, no need to be so vehement, it doesn't matter, does it?'

'Of *course* it matters. If I'd known that I'd never have let her do it. I'd have insisted on doing it myself.'

'But you couldn't have known that...'

'Oh, now look. Please. You *must* understand this. She had a history of mental illness, right? With that, there could *only* be one outcome to all this. She would go mad in the end. Christ, can't you *imagine* the strain? But I didn't know. Oh, look, you don't know it all yet. Maybe you'll see when I've told you the rest.'

'Okay, go on.'

'She was in hospital for nearly a year, and to start off with she was pretty violent. Attacked one of the doctors once. *Violent* mental illness! Can't you begin to see? If she was proved insane for the second time, *violently* insane, she would never, never get her freedom again. Do you see?'

'Oh. I think I'm beginning to. I didn't realise it was as bad as this.'

'No. Neither did I until it was too late.'

'Didn't anybody know?'

'Dan Hardisty found out in the end. But nobody knew then, or at least nobody thought of telling anyone who could have done something about it in time.'

'Who could have done anything?'

'I could. Anne, perhaps. Dan. I don't know.'

'Is there any more?'

'Yes. This is probably the most important bit of the lot. I want you to try and look at this situation from a child's point of view. Hilary's.'

'Yes?'

'Nearly five years old, with a happy, just about perfect home life. Suddenly her father is dying. Strangers in the place, sort of horrible, hushed atmosphere. I doubt if she was ever allowed to see her father. And her mother was wandering around the place looking like a ghost. Probably never played with her any more. Her whole life was sort of crumbling.'

'Yes?'

' "Yes? Yes?" ' she mimicked savagely. 'For God's sake, haven't you any imagination?'

'Look, bear with me, will you?' I said. 'Imagination I've got in plenty, but I haven't any children.'

'Okay, I'm sorry. Well, her father died. And then her

mother was taken away and Hilary was put in a home. Everything had collapsed about her and she wasn't even six years old.

'When Eileen came out of hospital she collected Hilary from that home, and that was when she realised what had been done to the child. So she did everything she could for her, to win back her confidence, you see. For over four years she lived for that child and she vowed that nothing would ever happen to hurt her again. Nothing at all.'

'And then Hilary was murdered.'

'Not only was Hilary murdered, but Eileen heard it all. She got that tape, remember? I don't understand why she didn't go mad there and then. But all that happened was that she blamed herself for leaving Hilary when she went into Wallington. Do you know why she went to see her solicitor that morning?'

'No.'

'She was setting up a trust for Hilary, to make sure that if *she* died suddenly the child would be all right.'

'Yes, that's a bit ironical, isn't it? Okay, I think I can see all that. Can you tell me what you talked about after Anne left?'

Diane looked at me helplessly, and sighed. 'So, you can see all that, can you? I don't think you can see *any* of that.'

She stood up and paced restlessly over to the window, where she stood gazing out over the sea. When at last she turned back to me her face was resigned and a small, twisted smile lifted the corner of her mouth.

'It must be my fault that you can't understand. Look, please try. This was the *second* time it had happened to Eileen, that the person she loved most in the world had died a horrible death, and in some way or other she had witnessed it both times.'

I think it was at about this time that I did begin to understand, and what had been to me a mere report of an interesting crime began to unfold as a dark and inevitable tragedy. Perhaps something of this showed in my face, for gradually Diane's expression softened, and she looked at me in a kindlier way.

'Do you begin to see it now?' she asked.

I nodded. 'Yes, I begin to see it now.'

She walked back to her chair and sat down again, relaxing and sighing as though some great task had been accomplished and a burden had been laid down. Which, perhaps, it had.

'I wanted you to understand,' she said quietly. 'There's no one except me now to fight Eileen's battles for her. Please, when you write all this, try to show her side of the story too.'

'I'll try.'

I have written that part of the conversation exactly as it happened. Diane, as she said, is a photographer and not a writer, but that was the story of her friend as she knew it, and as she had heard it from Eileen Denham, and that is how she fought Eileen's battle.

CHAPTER EIGHT

Diane made us a simple meal, a salad with ham and boiled eggs. Her attitude to me had changed, and I could see more of the woman I had known in London; sad, certainly, but friendly and frank, a good talker but a better listener. She set me to washing lettuce while she tossed a French dressing in a small jar, and we discussed the book I was trying to write, the form it would take, the characters I had met and those I would never meet.

'You know Pat Palmer?' she asked.

'I've met him.'

'Glamour boy, isn't he? Really makes me laugh. Did you get that Irish brogue? I thought so. Only puts it on when he wants to impress women. Dick Farley's different. I liked him.'

'Did you get to know them well?'

She put the jar down on the table, the smile fading from her face. 'They were very nice to us,' she said vaguely. 'Not what I'd expected.'

'Lots of questions, though?' I asked.

'You don't need to know all about that, do you? Please don't let's talk about it. It was a nightmare.'

'Okay. What I really do need to know is what you and Eileen talked about after Anne left.'

'Oh, yes, of course. I realise that. I'll try and remember. Let's leave it 'til after lunch.'

We talked of trivialities over lunch, books we had both read, people she had known in London and with whom I was still in touch: some fairly slanderous gossip crossed the table that day. We washed up, returned to the living room and sat down, and I switched on the tape recorder.

'Eileen saw Anne out,' she began, 'and then she came back and I asked her if she really meant to kill the man. She said yes, she really did, and I said that was fine by me, did she have any ideas? You know, I didn't know her well then, and for all I knew she might have had some cranky idea of finding out who'd done it before the police did, secret society Four Just Men sort of thing.'

'What sort of a state was she in at the time?'

Diane frowned. 'A lot of people might have thought she was very callous. Me too, I suppose. It didn't seem at first as if it had had any sort of effect on us. Maybe that was because we were both living alone, we didn't have to go through the conventional posturings. The truth is that it went too deep for that. I could see the strain in Eileen, and she could see it in me I expect, but nobody else would have noticed. You haven't got children, so I don't know if you'll understand this, it's a very primitive thing. There was a sort of savagery about it, controlled, but still there. Given something to direct it at, murder in this case, though I still don't think that word fits the case, we could be very patient and probably very cunning too. But in a way that took the place of normal grief, so maybe we seemed uncaring, unconcerned. I don't know. I never did care much about the impression I made on people, so maybe I just didn't notice.

'Well, Eileen hadn't got any stupid ideas. She knew that if anybody caught him it would be the police, and she wasn't about to waste her energy trying to beat them to it. Her idea at that time was to wait until the trial, then stand up in court and shoot him.

'I know you'll realise that was daft, but don't forget Eileen didn't know how difficult it is to hit someone with a revolver. All she had to go on was films and television, and of course they never seem to miss. She thought you could just go into a shop and buy a gun, too. I was quite surprised how ignorant she was about that.

'Well, as you know, I've done a bit of shooting and I was quite a fair shot. Not with a hand gun, though. It was rifles I'd used. I could see it was a rifle we'd need, but she'd never used one, so she didn't know.

'She'd never get near him with a gun, of course. I could just picture her trying to smuggle a rifle into court! It was going to have to be a long distance shot and that might be damned difficult to arrange. He'd be guarded so closely, you see, and it was no part of our plan to gun down some unfortunate policeman who happened to be standing beside him. But the chances were that the preliminary hearings would be in Hallerton.

'Now, I'd done some photography for postcards from the roof of one of those blocks of flats behind the courts in Hallerton, and I remembered you could see right down into the car park behind the court from there. About seven hundred yards it was, a hell of a distance, and I doubted if I could do it accurately enough from there, let alone Eileen. But we couldn't think of any other way. That was the only place where you could get a clear shot, there'd be crowds of police at ground level, you see.

'Anyway, what we agreed was that Eileen was to try and learn to shoot – and damned well, too – before he was caught. If she managed it, she'd use the gun. She'd already persuaded me on that, told me a bit about herself. But if she couldn't, and some people can't hit a barn if they're standing inside it no matter how hard they try, then I was to do it.

'That was all very well as far as it went, but we had two

big problems. Where was she going to learn to shoot and how was she going to get a gun? I couldn't teach her, the police aren't completely dumb, they'd only have to get wind of that and they'd pretty soon put two and two together, especially after Eileen's crazy escapade with Dan Hardisty's automatic; and we reckoned if either of us were to apply for a firearms permit in Hallerton we'd get a polite and very definite refusal. My own permit was years out of date. It took us quite a while to work out an answer.

'She had the idea in the end of going somewhere she wasn't known and getting a job with a gunsmith. That way she'd learn a bit, and it would seem quite natural she'd want to learn to shoot. A gunsmith would certainly be able to put her in touch with a rifle club, and she'd be known under a different name up there. She'd go back to her maiden name, Eileen MacNeil.

'It seemed a bit unlikely that she'd manage to get a job with a gunsmith. She'd really nothing to recommend her for it – except big blue eyes to use on the customers! But we couldn't think of anything better, so we decided that's what we'd try and if that didn't work we'd get together and think again. That was about it. I left a few minutes later.'

'What was your part in this?'

'Oh, yes, I'd forgotten all about that. Well, from what we knew of similar murder cases, the other one, that is, not what we were planning, which wasn't much at that time, it seemed unlikely that when an arrest was made it would be after a big car chase, you know – sirens, blazing guns, all the rest of it. It was much more probable it would all be very low key, and probably nothing even in the papers or on the radio until after the committal proceedings, which would be too late for us. We wouldn't have a cat in hell's chance once he was sent to the Assizes. So I was to go down to

London, different name again, and do freelance photography for the Press. That way I'd hear if anything happened before the general public did.'

'You didn't foresee any problems with that?'

She shook her head. 'I'm a good photographer,' she said simply. 'And I had a few contacts down there. They helped, and they kept quiet about my identity, too. I said I wanted to make a new life, and they were very nice. I felt a bit guilty about it.'

'You were good at your job while I knew you, anyway,' I said.

She smiled at me. 'Yes. And I did what I set out to do, too.'

It was to Brighton that Eileen had gone, taking with her only such personal belongings as she regarded as being strictly necessary. She had shut up the little house in the village, sold the pony and driven southwards with no clear knowledge of her destination. For some days she had driven around almost aimlessly, and had finally arrived in the popular seaside resort on a cold, rainy day in early June. She had left the car parked on the front at Marine Drive, and had walked across the shingle to gaze out over the grey foam and idly throw pebbles at the surging waves. Something about the town appealed to her, the anonymity of the busy streets and uncaring crowds perhaps, or the wild loneliness of the beach, deserted as it was in that bleak weather, and the crying of the gulls. She decided Brighton would suit her purpose and so, for the next few months, she disappeared into her new environment.

I returned to Brighton a few days later, after Diane had telephoned the gunsmith to ask him to see me. I found him in the dark shop, peering at me enquiringly over bi-focal spectacles, his white apron streaked with gun oil and a shot gun cradled lovingly in his arms.

'Oh, yes. You'll be the reporter,' he said when I introduced myself. 'Come into the back room and we'll talk.'

I looked curiously around the little workshop where Eileen Denham had spent so many hours. The fluorescent lighting was bright, without a tiring glare, and tools gleamed in its light, all clean and oiled and well cared for. Jackie Grey bustled about making tea while I wandered around and looked at the weapons in their racks on the walls, and he chatted about the weather and my journey south.

My eye was caught by a beautiful little antique pistol displayed in a mahogany wall case over the work bench. It gleamed and glinted in the light, polished and carefully maintained: no mere showpiece this, but a superb weapon treated with the skilful care it merited.

There was a card propped in the corner of the glass case, and I leaned across the bench to read it.

'To Jackie, with love and gratitude. Eileen.'

The handwriting was upright and rounded, childish perhaps, but clear and legible. The card, like the case and the gun, had been recently dusted.

I turned, and was surprised to see Mr Grey was looking at the gun, his lip trembling slightly and his eyes misty. He caught my glance, and smiled apologetically.

'A good gun,' he said huskily. 'I leave it there so I can look at it when I'm working.'

I nodded, and asked a trite question about the rifle in the vice in an effort to pass over the difficult moment. It was an unfortunate choice.

'Yes, that's right. That's not Eileen's gun, but it's the same.

96

Lee Enfield 7.62, converted from the .303. One of the best rifles ever made if you know what you're doing with it.'

I nodded again, and he smiled and poured the tea carefully. He pushed my cup along the bench towards me.

'Now, what can I tell you?'

'First of all, why did you give Eileen a job?'

He stirred his tea thoughtfully, took off his glasses, and polished them on the hem of his apron.

'I'd been needing a bit of help. Just part time, to help keep the shop clean and do the paperwork. I'm no good at accounts myself, so I put a little notice in the window. One or two people tried it, but they weren't much good. Not very reliable. So I just about gave up, but I left the notice in the window just in case.

'Then Eileen came in one afternoon and asked for the job. I wasn't too sure about it, she'd never done shop work before, or accounts, but I said she could come for a week and see how she managed. She did very well, so she stayed.'

'Just part time?'

He laughed. 'It was meant to be part time, but she spent more time here than anywhere else. You see, she'd a feel for the job. She liked guns, not just for what they were, but for the feel of them and the look. She didn't know anything, you understand, but she could tell a good gun. She liked to handle them. At first she was just in the shop, selling a bit sometimes or keeping the books straight, but it wasn't long before she was helping in here too. Just simple bits of cleaning at first.'

He chuckled suddenly, and leaned back, clasping his hands behind his head and crossing his legs.

'Unscrupulous, she was, in that shop. Flattery, that's how she did it. Get an old fellow in the shop and she'd hand over the most expensive gun in stock, and say that was probably more the sort of thing he was used to. Or a younger chap, if he couldn't make up his mind between two guns, if the heavier one was the dearest, she'd suggest it was too much for him to handle, and he'd buy it just to show her, or if it was the lighter one she'd just hint that a light trigger was perhaps for a more *experienced* man, you know, and he'd take it for the same reason. She really made me laugh, she could have sold a Bible to a blind atheist.'

I smiled. 'When did she first start learning about guns in earnest?' I asked.

'Oh, it wasn't long. She started off just doing a bit of cleaning and oiling, but she was keen to learn, you under-stand, and I didn't mind teaching her what I could. I like talking about my work and she was a very good listener. Two weeks, maybe, and she could strip down a simple mechanism and put it back together again. I always checked her work, of course, but it was a bad day if I had to do it over again.'

'And then she wanted to learn to shoot?'

'Yes.' The smile faded from his face. 'Ah, well. It seemed natural enough. That was what she was after all the time, I know that now. But say what you like, Eileen was always good with guns. If she ever gets over her trouble she can come back and work here, and be welcome. For all she went wrong, poor girl.'

There was a long silence while he gazed sadly at the little gun on the wall, stirring his tea automatically, a small, wistful smile on his lips. Then he glanced at me, coughed apolo-getically, and straightened up.

'Yes,' he said briskly. 'She wanted to shoot. Well, we got her a permit, no bother there, she gave me as one reference and a friend she had in London for another. The police here know me, so her permit came through with no bother. And I've plenty of friends in rifle clubs, so she went with them a couple of weekends. Started off on a .22, but she wasn't long on that. Went on to a 7.62 and bought the Lee Enfield. She'd used it a few times, liked it, so I said she could have it cheap.'

'Tell me, Mr Grey...'

'Not Mr Grey. Just Jackie.'

'All right, Jackie. Thank you. Tell me, how did she learn so fast?'

'Ah, well, it wasn't just the weekends she was over. Rob Dilley, the man who owns the farm where they shoot, he was very taken with Eileen. Said she could go over any time for a bit of practice. Most evenings she was away in that big car for a shot or two. Rob must have forgotten about farming those evenings, but don't go and see him. He was very upset when it happened, and he wouldn't take kindly to questions.'

'No, I won't.'

'Thank you. Well, you'll have heard there are born good shots and made good shots. Now, Eileen wasn't a born good shot, she had to work at it, but she worked hard and she got very good in the end. When that friend of hers, Diane, came up for a few days that autumn they went shooting, and there wasn't much to choose between them, for all Diane had done plenty of shooting before and won cups and all for it. Mind you, Diane was using a strange gun, but there wasn't that much in it. We had a drink that evening for a celebration.'

'Did you know anything about Eileen's past?'

He shook his head.

'I knew she was a widow and had a child that died. She didn't want to talk about it, and I'm not one for prying. She'd had trouble she was trying to forget. That was good enough for me. And it always will be at that. I just hope she'll come home here one day.'

99

'Do you have any contact with her now?'

'I write a letter now and then. She doesn't answer, but I don't expect that yet. Maybe she'll write one day.'

He relapsed into silence, and I felt it was time to go.

'Jackie, I was talking to Diane the other day.'

'Yes?'

'She told me Eileen had been very happy working here.'

He smiled, and nodded. 'Yes. Thank you.'

I left him staring at the little antique gun, and the card in the corner of the case.

'To Jackie, with love and gratitude.   Eileen.'

CHAPTER NINE

Summer drifted thunderously into autumn, a wild season that year with sudden storms, rain and gales, moving up and down the country.

Brighton was cold, bleak and dirty, like any summer resort in the autumn, paper blowing wetly down the gutters, billboard posters streaked, grimy and peeling. Sea mists rolled in from the Channel at night, thick and heavy, muffling sounds and dimming the lights.

Eileen would arrive at the shop late in the morning, and stay sometimes far into the night listening to Jackie as he worked at his bench and talked, as much to himself as to her, of the guns he loved. Perhaps she would have an oil can in her hand, or a polishing cloth, sometimes she would be sanding a walnut stock that he had shaped, or be putting the final polish to it after he had carved it, each one individually, with a pheasant, a design of leaves, or a stag's head.

Sometimes in that gentle setting she would forget the misery of her life, her increasing struggle against the bleak mists that so often gripped her mind, leaving her confused and terrified. Late in the night, when she could not sleep, she would sit at the window of her tiny flat, rigid, her thoughts racing in an uncontrollable turmoil as she stared unseeingly over the bright lights and black shadows of the town.

If Jackie noticed the strain she was undergoing he said nothing, his instinctive good manners leaving her white, thin face, the eyes huge and black ringed, the cheeks hollow, her continual loss of weight, unremarked, but all the time his kindliness helped her, and she was soothed and comforted by the unchanging slow pace of his work and life. Sometimes he would look across at her as she sat dreaming on the bench, his shrewd old eyes anxious and concerned, but he made no comment, never questioned her, never let her see his fears. Occasionally he would buy her little presents; a lace handkerchief, an old engraving he had seen in an antique shop, and often there would be a small bottle of whisky tucked into her pocket just as she was leaving, a brief request that she drink his health before she turned in, and a wish, more sincere than she imagined, that she should have a good night.

When she was on the rifle range her determination to do well overcame any other emotions she might have felt as she lay on the ground, her cheek pressed against the comforting hardness of the stock, staring through the accurate aperture sight at the cross-hairs aligned on the target. Rob Dilley, her patient instructor, proud of her progress and increasingly attracted by her, would sometimes remark on her thinness, but she would merely smile, make a light comment on the prevailing fashion, and turn the subject with a question about filters, or a request to borrow a book.

She maintained her rifle meticulously and, from tips she had picked up from Rob or read from books, prepared it for its eventual deadly purpose. A strip of matt black tape down the barrel to prevent glare, gleaned from a book on snipers in Vietnam, was noticed with amusement by the other members of the team. The thin line of white paint on the front sight for easier aiming in poor light went unremarked; many of them used this technique.

Diane Clayton came to Brighton for a week at the beginning of October. She was horrified when she saw Eileen, who put on an unconvincing display of bright good humour, and spoke of a bad attack of influenza to account for her wraithlike appearance. Diane went back to London, impressed with Eileen's ability with a rifle, but disturbed and uneasy about her health. From that time on she telephoned frequently for long conversations, and Eileen became increasingly grateful for her friendship and support.

It was on a Saturday morning in early November that Anne Butler rang up. Eileen was lying on her bed, tossing in a restless, nightmarish sleep, when the telephone rang. She awoke, shuddering, and reached for the receiver.

'Hallo?'

'Eileen?'

She did not recognise the breathless voice at the other end of the telephone, and she frowned in puzzlement.

'Yes?'

'Anne. Anne Butler. I said I'd telephone. You'd better come up now if you want to.'

'What's happened?'

There was an uneasy pause.

'Well,' said Anne at last, 'what you wanted to know.'

'Can somebody hear you?'

'Yes.'

'I'll call at the shop when I get there.'

'No!' The reply came quickly. 'No, don't do that. Ring me here. It'll be all right then. I'll wait.' She hung up abruptly.

Mechanically, Eileen carried out the actions she had planned so carefully, telephoning Jackie Grey and Rob Dilley with the story of a sudden illness of a friend in the north, rolling the rifle in brown paper, padded to disguise the distinctive shape, slipping three carefully prepared cartridges into the pocket of her jacket, cartridges with two crossed grooves carved across the copper nose of the bullet, which would cause the bullet to spread on impact, leaving a gaping exit hole.

At the door she hesitated and then turned back to the mantelpiece, took down a small photograph of a grave-faced, dark-haired child, glanced at it briefly and slid it into her pocket.

The motorway was almost deserted north of London, and Eileen made good time to Hallerton, and arrived in the afternoon. She stopped on the outskirts of the town and rang Anne from a telephone box.

'He's on the moor.' The voice was tense and breathless. 'There's a big search on. He tried it again and got spotted. I don't know anything more. Goodbye.' There was a click, and a moment later the dialling tone sounded. Eileen slowly replaced the receiver.

She parked the Jaguar in a shallow, abandoned quarry in the side of a hill, and climbed out, looking around slowly at the coppery sky, at the hills standing out unnaturally sharply and clearly. She shivered suddenly, and turned to the rock face. Quickly, she climbed the steep slope, reaching for hand holds and moving surely and swiftly. When she reached the top she looked out across the rolling moor to the main road, listening to the hum of the traffic. Even from where she stood over a mile away she could see the bright twinkle of the police cars' blue lamps, parked at the side of the road, from where the drivers scanned the passing traffic.

He would stay away from the main road. They would have to bring him back along the little side road she had used.

She turned slowly, and gazed out over the surrounding countryside.

No beauty spot, this moor. Bleak and desolate in winter, in summer the dust and dry grass were littered with rubbish which blew drearily and hopelessly through the stunted bushes. The scrubland stretched away to low, black hills in the distance, outlined sharply against the lurid sky.

About two miles away, Eileen could see a line of searchers, moving slowly across the hills. She stared at them for a moment, and then turned away.

On the horizon, a rolling bank of threatening black clouds was gathering, looming ominously.

The sharp drone of a helicopter made her start and look up quickly. It swung towards her, dropped, and then rose sharply and whirred away, the pilot reassured by a closer look at the solitary figure standing on the scree.

Hoofbeats thudded away to the left of her, and she looked down to see a mounted policeman cantering fast along the broad grass verge by the little road. She watched him as he rode away behind the hill and turned back to look at the line of searchers.

Away in the distance, the sound of a siren cut through the still air. From the black clouds, now rolling towards the moors, came a threatening rumble and the skies suddenly grew darker.

Eileen shivered violently, turned away and scrambled quickly back down the rock face.

The shadows in the quarry were a hard, dark black. Everything stood out in sharp contrast. It was a strange, eerie sight.

Slowly, Eileen walked round to the boot of the car. She pressed the catch, reached into the boot and stripped the brown paper from the rifle. She picked it up, ran her hands down the slender, deadly shape admiring, as always, the beauty of the economical and workmanlike lines. She reached into her pocket for the cartridges, slid the magazine out of the gun and began to load it.

Everything had taken on a familiar, dream-like quality.

The thunder rumbled again, closer now.

Eileen's fingers faltered, a cartridge slipped from the

magazine and rolled under the car. She ignored it and pushed the magazine home.

The muffled throb of the helicopter echoed from the rock face, and she raised her head slowly to look up through the gathering dusk as it flew overhead, swung away then flew back towards the sunset.

Eileen slipped the strap of the rifle over her shoulder and turned back to the rock face.

A few miles away, Hardisty raised the binoculars to his eyes, leaned back against the police car and swung them in a slow arc over the horizon. He adjusted the focus slightly, fingers light on the knurled wheel, and lowered them to look up as the helicopter roared overhead, sideslipped, then wheeled back over the road.

A police car speeded up the road towards him and swung into the layby. Palmer jumped out, the car pulled away and drove on down the road. Hardisty raised his eyebrows questioningly as Palmer walked towards him shaking his head, and they both turned back to scan the surrounding moors.

'If I hadn't seen that bloody car with my own eyes I'd swear this bastard didn't exist,' commented Palmer bitterly.

Hardisty raised the binoculars again and swept them across the skyline.

'How's the kid?' he asked.

'Still unconscious. She's concussed.'

'That all?'

'Yes. We got there in time, just for once.' Palmer looked up at the dark sky, his eyes narrowed calculatingly.

'How long do you think this'll hold off?' he asked.

Hardisty put down the binoculars and glanced up briefly.

'Not much longer. What's this guy done, tunnelled his way out?'

'God knows. It's going to be no fun at all, looking for him in a storm.'

Hardisty looked back over his shoulder. 'Here they come,' he commented briefly.

About forty men were outlined starkly against the sky, moving slowly towards them in an evenly spaced line as they beat the thick bushes that might afford cover from the searching helicopters.

The car radio crackled briefly, and the young constable reached for the microphone and acknowledged. After a moment he replaced it on the hook and leaned out of the window.

'The helicopters are going in now, sir. They don't want to be caught up there in a storm, I reckon.'

'Okay,' replied Hardisty, and glanced at Palmer, who shrugged.

'I am not going to enjoy reading about this,' he said.

'Me neither,' agreed Hardisty, raising the binoculars again.

'I wonder if we trampled him to death in the rush.'

Hardisty grinned.

'It's not funny,' reproved Palmer.

'Hell, if I don't laugh about this I'll cry.'

They both looked up as the thud of hoofbeats met their ears, and two mounted policemen rode around the corner, and reined in at the sight of them.

'No sign, sir.'

'Keep trying.'

Palmer stared after them resentfully as they trotted across the road and cantered up the rise on the other side.

A sudden streak of lightning blazed across the black sky, and flashed against the hills as the thunder crashed and echoed across the moor. The rain hissed against the grass, and suddenly the full force of the storm was upon them.

They dived into the car, the driver turned the ignition key and switched on the windscreen wipers.

'How about that?' muttered Palmer bitterly, staring through the streaming windscreen at the road, where the water was already running down the shallow gutters.

The lightning blazed again, the thunder rumbled, black clouds rolling menacingly.

'Surely it's too heavy to last?' asked Hardisty.

'Don't you believe it, sir.' The driver's Midland accent was very pronounced. 'This could go on all night.'

Another flash of lightning almost directly in front of them blinded them for a moment, and as their eyes recovered a car pulled into the layby beside them, its headlights dipped, blue lamp flashing.

The driver wound down his window and shouted from the other car. 'Radios aren't working. Is Sergeant Palmer there?'

Palmer leaned forward. 'What is it?'

'Can you come with us, sir? Somebody thinks they saw him doubling back to the main road. Is Mr Hardisty with you?'

'Yes.'

'There'll be a car along in a few minutes. Can you take charge of a party down at Hamble Farm?'

'Okay.'

'I didn't think we'd be allowed to stay out of the rain for long.' Palmer sounded resigned as he stepped out of the car. 'Tell mother I died despondent and soaking wet.'

The car drove away down the road, the tyres swishing through the running water.

Hardisty leaned forward and put his elbows on the back of the seat, his chin cupped in his hands.

'How many men out there now?' he asked.

'About four hundred, I reckon. Warraton and West Faring are in on this too.'

'Think he's got away?'

The driver shrugged. 'I don't see how he can have. He's on foot, and he didn't have time to reach the roads before we did. I reckon we had him surrounded within half an hour.'

A sudden gust of wind rocked the car and the rain drummed violently on to the roof, almost drowning the driver's voice.

'I'm glad we're not on foot!'

Hardisty winced as a sheet of lightning momentarily dazzled him, and turned his head as a car drew up alongside, the sound of its engine smothered by the roar of the rain.

'Good luck, sir,' said the driver as Hardisty ducked out of the car, turning up his collar as he did so.

Hamble Farm was only two miles away. The car travelled quickly, the windscreen wipers working against the blinding rain, the tyres sliding helplessly on the treacherous surface at the corners.

It was five o'clock when they arrived. The storm had made it nearly pitch dark, and the men were shrouded in heavy waterproof capes and carrying torches. There were two dogs with the group sitting by their handlers, occasionally standing up to shake the water out of their dripping coats.

Hardisty jumped out of the car, and strode across to the barn where most of the men were sheltering, sipping cups of scalding coffee that a kindly woman from the farm had brought out.

'Dan!'

He turned quickly to see Stewart standing in a corner holding a large scale map against a wall. He walked over and Stewart pointed to the map.

109

'Look, he's been seen there, about two miles from the road. He may try to get back along there,' his finger traced a line on the squared map, 'so we want that bit covered. Spread across from there and keep the torches moving. We should trap him up by the crossroads.'

By the time Hardisty and his men left the farm and spread across the area allocated to them the wind had risen to gale force and the rain was driving into their faces with almost demoniacal savagery. Lightning still blazed intermittently and the thunder rumbled from the hills.

Bent almost double against the wind, the men struggled up the steep banks of the road and, torches swinging to cover every inch of the ground, began to fight their way across the scrubby moor.

They had been walking for about half an hour when word was passed to Hardisty that a car had been found in a quarry off the road. The sergeant who brought the message had to shout to make his voice heard over the screaming wind.

'There's a car down in the quarry.'

Hardisty stopped, and turned towards him.

'So?' he yelled.

'Shall we put a guard on it?' The policeman wiped a hand across his streaming face and leaned into the wind as Hardisty replied.

'Why? Isn't it locked?'

'It's an open car. Jaguar XK 120.'

'A *what*?'

'Jaguar XK 120. An open sports job.'

Hardisty stared at him. After a moment he turned and looked back towards the quarry.

'Where's the driver?'

His voice was lost in the wind, and the policeman leaned towards him. Hardisty shook his head.

'Never mind, I'll go down. You take over here, keep them in a straight line, about ten feet apart.'

When Hardisty reached the quarry he could not see the car at first. The streaming rain hid almost everything from view, and even the powerful torch he carried could not penetrate that grey curtain.

Then a flash of lightning illuminated the entire rock face in a stark blaze and the green car, gleaming sleekly in the light, stood out brilliantly against the black rocks.

He walked over to it, and ran his hand along the sweeping wing, frowning as he tried to remember any distinguishing marks that could dispel his doubt and replace it with certainty. He walked around the car, playing his torch over it as he did so. When he reached the back he shone the beam on to the number plate, and racked his memory for the occasional glimpses he had previously had of the car.

The torch beam dropped, and the sudden glint of metal behind the rear wheel caught his eye, and made him stoop swiftly for a closer look.

He stood up, the cartridge in his hand, his fist clenching on it convulsively. There was no doubt in his mind now and his face whitened with the implications.

He swung the beam of the torch up the rock face, his eyes narrowed against the rain, his head turning to follow the blade of light as it crossed and recrossed the broken surface.

The torch beam was swamped suddenly by the glare of a pair of powerful headlights, and Hardisty spun round in surprise. The lights dipped, he saw the blue lamp on the roof and walked forward.

The driver's door opened, and a sergeant stepped out as he approached.

'Been called off, sir,' the policeman shouted.

Hardisty stopped, and turned his torch back into the quarry. 'Why?'

'Don't know, the radio's not working well enough to hear. I think they've got him.'

The wind died suddenly, and the rain hissed viciously, and then faded to a fine mist. The silence was almost startling.

Hardisty and the sergeant glanced up at the sky almost simultaneously and then turned as another car swept into the quarry behind them.

Palmer stepped out and walked over towards them. Hardisty flashed his torch, and the detective turned his head and put up a hand to shade his eyes.

'Turn that bloody thing off,' he snapped irritably.

Hardisty did so, and waited for him to come up.

'What the hell's going on?' he demanded.

'We've got him.' Palmer's voice was a mixture of fury and frustration. 'For what it's worth. He's nothing more than a stupid hit and run driver.'

'*What?*'

'He's Polish or something, I don't know. Hasn't been over here long anyway. Hit the kid, thought he'd killed her, panicked, piled her in the car and took off. By the time he realised his mistake we were all after him.'

The sergeant swore under his breath. Hardisty stared at Palmer.

'Where is he now?'

'On his way back to Wallington hospital. He tripped and broke his ankle or something. You coming back with me?'

Hardisty glanced back over his shoulder into the quarry.

'No, you go on,' he said. 'I'll follow you later.'

'Suit yourself.' Palmer turned away.

'Oh, Pat?'

'Yes?'

'Which way are they taking him to Wallington?'

'Down the main road.'

'Not past here?'

'No. Why?'

Hardisty shook his head. 'It doesn't matter.'

Palmer looked at him curiously for a moment. Then he shrugged and turned back to the car.

As it pulled away out of the quarry the sergeant looked at Hardisty narrowly.

'There won't be many more cars going back this way,' he warned. 'Most of them are on the main road.'

Hardisty smiled. 'Don't worry, I'll get home.'

He watched the car swing out of the quarry, then turned and walked back to the Jaguar. He leaned against the door and lit a cigarette, cupping his hands around the match and gratefully drawing the smoke into his lungs.

The lightning flashed again and only seconds later the thunder roared. Hardisty looked up at the clouds scudding across the sky, then carefully scanned the black outlines of the rocks.

The wind whispered briefly and died again. Two cars drove past the quarry, the noise of the engines fading into the night.

The lightning flickered again and the rocks gleamed with reflected light. The thunder was a muted rumble away over the hills.

Hardisty finished his cigarette and threw the butt down into the stones at his feet, where it glowed redly for a moment, then hissed and died. He stood up, and threw back his head.

'Eileen!' he called, and the rocks echoed his voice mockingly.

'Eileen! ... 'leen! ... 'een!'

'All right, you can come out now. We've got him.'

The echoes died, and the wind moaned and sobbed, throwing a brief spatter of rain lightly over the car and the man standing beside it. The lightning cracked again, and blue flames flashed across the rocks, blazing and flaring angrily as the thunder crashed and roared directly overhead; the wind screamed suddenly and then howled into a wild diminuendo, dying away over the hills.

She was standing in front of him, her face a pale blur, her eyes huge in the gloom. Hardisty stared at her as she stood there, unmoving, the rifle slung carelessly across her shoulders. Her black hair streamed across her face, she raised her head slowly and looked back across the quarry to the bleak outline of the rocks against the sky, where a star shone serenely between the ragged edges of the wild black clouds.

'Give me that gun.' His voice was quiet and controlled, and for a moment he thought she had not heard him. Then she turned her head slowly back towards him, and reached up to her shoulder, the strap of the rifle slipping down her arm, her hand reaching for the stock.

The thunder growled a muted warning, and a streak of blue fire hurtled across the quarry and flared on the rocks as the thunder roared in a wild cacophony, echoing deafeningly from the rock face, and crashing across the hill.

Eileen screamed and threw up her arm to protect her eyes.

The rifle cracked.

The thunder died away suddenly, and the air was still. Then a quiet wind whispered softly over the moors, and the crescent moon gleamed coolly through the torn storm clouds.

Eileen lowered her arm and stared blindly at the man by the car, her eyes glazed with fear and shock as he turned his head and raised a hand to his shoulder, where the bullet had ripped through the heavy cloth of his coat, slamming him back against the rocks before smashing into the quarry behind him and whining away into the distance.

Eileen drew a deep, shuddering breath. He stepped forward as she swayed towards him and caught her, pulling her to her feet and holding her against him as her head dropped to his shoulder. She sighed, leaning against him, the rifle slipping unheeded to the ground beside them.

For long moments they stood. At last Eileen raised her head and stared up into his face, her eyes wide and drenched with tears.

'I nearly killed you,' she whispered.

He stroked her hair gently, and pulled her head back against his chest, holding her against him as he ran his lips lightly across her forehead. She caught her breath, and pressed her hands against his shoulders.

'Oh, I'm so sorry!'

'It doesn't matter.'

She felt very small and defenceless pressed against him, and he put his arms around her shaking shoulders and hugged her to him as though she were a frightened child. She raised her head slowly and looked up at him, her eyes huge in the pale moonlight.

He looked down at her for a moment, his face grave and thoughtful. Then he bent his head and kissed her lips lightly, his eyes fixed on hers. Her lashes fluttered, her eyes closed and she sighed. He kissed her again, his lips brushing gently against hers. Slowly, she reached up a hand and rested it against his cheek, and he leaned his head into it as she smiled tremblingly and opened her eyes.

After a long moment he raised his head and looked around.

'Come on,' he said quietly. 'Let's go home.'

*   *   *

It was after midnight when Hardisty drove into the mews and pulled up in front of the door. Eileen looked around as he switched off the engine and swung out of the car, reaching for the rifle as he did so. He unlocked the door and turned back to her.

'Come on.'

She shivered as she walked into the room and jumped as he slammed the door behind her. When she turned he was looking down at her, his face hard and unsmiling.

'Go and have a hot bath.'

'What about you?'

He ignored her, sat down in the armchair and began to strip down the rifle without looking at her again.

After a moment she turned away.

He worked quickly, cleaning and oiling the gun. When she came out of the bathroom wrapped in a towel he was locking it away in the steel cabinet on the wall.

'That's my gun,' she said quietly.

He looked at her, his face expressionless. 'Go to bed.'

'What about you?' she asked again.

'I'll be along later.'

She looked at him fearfully. 'What are you going to do?' she whispered.

He rounded on her, his face twisted with anger.

'What do you think I'm going to do?' he demanded savagely. 'I'm going to get dry. Is that all right?'

He walked out of the room, and slammed the door behind him. Eileen shivered again, and turned away into the bedroom.

She woke later from a restless sleep, startled by something she had dreamed or heard, sitting up quickly looking fearfully around her.

Hardisty was sitting smoking in a chair by the window, the first light of dawn reflected palely on his white shirt, the cigarette glowing between his lips. He turned his head slowly and looked at her. After a moment she sighed and lay down again, turning away and falling instantly into a dream-haunted sleep.

Black, rolling moors. Skeleton trees throwing dead, grey branches up to the red sky and she wandered, searching hopelessly, desperately for something she had lost. A gaping cavern, and she turned into it. Robin Denham's skull-like face loomed over her, huge and cadaverous, twisted in a final, agonised paroxysm, his lips parting to speak to her, and she strained to hear what he would say. But from his mouth issued instead, terrifying, the heartrending screams of her dying child, and she shrieked in a wild protest, howling and screaming in a hopeless attempt to drown the cries that would forever echo in her mind.

'Eileen! Honey, come on now...'

'Oh, God! Oh, no, HILARY!'

'Come on, baby. It's over. It's gone now.'

Hands on her shoulders, demanding, insistent, a voice speaking urgently. Her eyes flew open, hands clasped frantically over her ears, teeth bared in an anguished, animal snarl.

'Okay, baby, wake up. It's gone. It was a dream.'

Shuddering and gasping she stared at him, the wild light in her eyes fading with dawning recognition.

'Dan?'

'Yeah, only Dan. It's all over now.'

'Oh, God. Oh, Dan, I had a dream, I...'

'Yeah, I know. Don't talk now. Lie still, honey, just relax, I'm here.'

She turned her head into his hand, shaking, teeth clenched

in remembered fear. He stroked the hair from her eyes, gentle, soothing, tense with pity.

'Oh, baby,' he whispered. 'What have you done to yourself?'

'Don't go, Dan. Please don't go!'

'I'll stay. Don't worry, I'm here.'

He lay down beside her, cradling her in his arms, holding her head against his shoulder, and speaking gently, until at last she lay still and fell into the deep sleep of total exhaustion.

CHAPTER TEN

Eileen's cheeks were flushed and feverish, her forehead damp with sweat, and she tossed and moaned uneasily. Hardisty, having failed to waken her, telephoned for a doctor, who shook his head doubtfully.

'Malnutrition,' he said at last. 'Shock maybe. Don't like this fever. She ought to be in hospital.'

'She's in a pretty shaky mental state at the moment. She might get worse if she wakes up in a strange place.'

'Hmm. Well, we'll see how it goes. I'll come back this afternoon. If she wakes up, get her to drink. Plenty of soup, milk, that sort of thing. Got to get some nourishment into her.'

'She can stay here?'

The doctor looked at him over the top of his spectacles. 'She needs constant attendance.'

'That's okay.'

'She can stay for now. I'm promising nothing. We'll see how she is this afternoon.'

Hardisty telephoned Walshe. 'I'm sick,' he said uncompromisingly.

'Me too,' said Walshe. 'What's the matter with you?'

'I'm dying.'

'Okay, I'll send you a wreath. Come back and haunt us after the funeral.'

Hardisty grinned. 'Should be about a week. That okay?'

'Yes. That gives me plenty of time to think up some really horrible job for you.'

Eileen awoke briefly at about noon and lay silently, staring up at the ceiling. Hardisty spoke to her, and she looked at him uncomprehendingly, making no reply. He brought her a mug of soup, which she drank, and he bathed her face. She lay resistless, and when he told her to go back to sleep, docilely closed her eyes.

The doctor was non-committal.

'She can stay for the present,' was all he would say. 'Remember, plenty of nourishing liquids. I'll be back tomorrow.'

On the second day Palmer called round to see Hardisty, found the door unlocked and walked in. He stood at the bedroom door. Hardisty looked up and waited for the inevitable comment.

Palmer walked over, and looked down at Eileen, unconscious and feverish on the bed.

'Christ!' he said softly.

Hardisty did not reply, and Palmer looked at him quizzically.

'Hope you know what you're doing, boyo!'

'So do I.'

Palmer grinned. 'Don't worry, I'll back up your story. If anybody asks me what's the matter with you I'll tell them you've got the pox.'

'Fuck off,' said Hardisty amicably.

On the fourth day, Eileen spoke for the first time.

'Dan?'

He looked round in surprise. 'Well, hallo there, sleepyhead!'

'Have I been ill?'

He walked over and sat on the bed beside her.

'Not so's you'd notice. Been in a coma for four days.'

'Oh.'

'Drink your milk and go back to sleep.'

Obediently, she drank the glass of milk he gave her and lay down, closing her eyes. He sat and watched until she was asleep.

She recovered quickly after that and was soon up and sitting in the living room for short periods. The doctor called less frequently, but spoke to her severely when he did so.

'You eat plenty now,' he warned her. 'You're in a disgusting state and it's your own fault. Don't let it happen again.'

She listened to his strictures, and looked ruefully at Hardisty after he left.

'Serve you right,' he grinned.

'I suppose so.' She wandered across the room, and sat on the arm of his chair, resting her cheek on the top of his head.

'Why are you so good to me?'

'I dunno. Must be this habit you have of fainting at my feet. Can't resist it.'

'I've never fainted at your feet.'

'No, I've always caught you, haven't I? Shan't next time. I'll just let you fall. Splat.'

She smiled, and he looked up at her and put his arm round her waist.

'When have you got to go back to work?' she asked.

'Last week.'

She took his wrist, and looked at his watch. 'You're going to be late.'

He laughed. 'Go back to bed.'

'I'm not tired. I'll go soon.' She stood up and walked over to the window. He watched her in silence for a while.

'That night up on the moor,' he said at last. 'You really meant to kill him?'

She did not reply, and after a moment he went on.

'Real pistol-packin' momma, aren't you? Must be a crack

shot, too. Pitch dark, and a howling gale. How were you going to do it? You have a little radar set up there maybe?'

'I don't want to talk about it.'

'I'll just bet you don't!' he said explosively. 'Like it or not, you're going to do just that. White paint on the front sight, taped barrel, dum dum bullets. Real little professional, aren't you? Oh yes, and just tell me something, will you? How would you know which one to shoot? Assuming you could see them, that is?'

'The others would have been in uniform.'

'Oh really? Well, I could name you at least a dozen from Hallerton alone who weren't in uniform, and there were two other forces out there as well. Maybe sixty in plain clothes. Me for one. How about that? I could have been blasted down in the prime of life and never known anything about it.'

'You're not in the prime of life.'

'Don't try and evade the issue, baby.' He stood up and began to pace up and down the room. 'You could have killed somebody up there that night, and you're going to have to face that.'

'Why don't you save the third degree for your job?'

He stopped, and looked across the room at her.

'Okay,' he said, 'shall we do that? I'll go back to work right now. And I'll take you with me. We'll go into a little room somewhere. We'll be sitting on opposite sides of a table and I'll be asking a lot of very awkward questions. Starting off with what you were doing up there that night with a rifle? Where you got it. How you learned to use it. You didn't know anything about guns six months ago. And you'd stay behind bars until I got the answers. Would you like that?'

She shivered.

'No, I didn't think you would. Oh, and there's just one

thing you ought to know. If you had shot anyone you'd have killed an innocent man. He wasn't the one you were after, he was a hit and run driver.'

She turned and looked at him uncomprehendingly. 'What?'

'You heard me.'

'You don't use helicopters to get a hit and run driver!'

'Oh, we didn't know. We thought the same as you. I wouldn't mind knowing how you found out about it, either. Where were you, Brighton, wasn't it? We didn't find out the truth until we caught him. Just as well that didn't happen anywhere near you, right?'

She stared at him, wide-eyed, lips moving wordlessly.

'Quite a thought, isn't it?' he said.

'Then you haven't got him,' she whispered. 'It's all still going on.'

'It's all over where you're concerned,' he said. 'Don't you think any different.'

Her eyes dropped, and she shook her head. 'I thought it was all finished. But he still hasn't been caught.'

He looked at her in silence, his expression softening. 'Honey?'

'Yes?'

'Look, I'm not angry with you. Maybe I can understand how you feel. But we've got to talk about it.'

She turned back to the window and leaned against the frame, staring out over the roofs into the evening sky.

'Why don't you just arrest me and get it over with? That's what you're planning to do, isn't it?'

'You think so?'

She glanced at him briefly, and shrugged.

'I'd have a few awkward questions to answer myself, wouldn't I?' he said.

'That wouldn't stop you.'

'Maybe not.' He sat on the arm of a chair, and offered her a cigarette. She shook her head, and he lit one for himself.

'No, Eileen, that's not what I'm planning. I don't say I'll never do it, that depends on you. I hope it won't be necessary.'

'You want me to promise I'll never do it again?'

'You'd promise anything under threats.'

'What, then?'

He drew on his cigarette, and exhaled the smoke slowly.

'You bought a gun, and you learned how to use it. I'm not asking how, not yet anyway, but I know why. So it wasn't just an unpremeditated impulse like the last time. You planned this. Okay, I can see the motive, I can sympathise, but just what are you hoping to gain by it?'

'Gain?'

'Yes. Have you looked any further at it? Let's say we catch him, which is getting increasingly unlikely, and you manage to kill him. Again, pretty unlikely, but say you do it. What then?'

She shrugged. 'He'd be dead.'

He waited, but she said no more.

'Is that all?'

'Yes.'

'What about you? Ten, fifteen years in jail. Have you thought about that? Would it be worth it?'

'Yes.'

'Have you thought about it?' he insisted.

She did not reply.

'Why do you want to kill him?' he asked quietly.

'He killed Hilary. And the others.'

'Killing him isn't going to bring them back. It's too late now. When did you start planning this?'

'A few days after I saw you.'

'That's a long time ago. Maybe it seemed like a good idea then, but now? You've got nothing to prove, Eileen. I know how you felt about Hilary. Maybe I'd feel the same way if somebody killed Terry, but this isn't going to help.'

'After six months, you think I'm going to give up just because you say so?'

'No. I just want you to think about it and make the decision on your own. I'll talk about it if you like, if that'll help, I can't do any more than that. But I'll make damned sure you can't kill him even if you decide to try. If we get him you'll be watched for every minute, day and night, right up to the time he's in jail.'

'How will you do that?'

'I'll tell Bill Walshe all about it. He'll fix it.'

'And you say you're not going to arrest me. You won't have to, will you? Somebody else can do the dirty work.'

'No, I don't think they'll do that. They might, but I wouldn't think so. The situation probably won't arise anyway. We're not getting very far on this case.'

'You don't think he'll be caught?'

'No. I think he's moved out of the area now. Maybe even out of the country.'

She looked at him steadily. 'No problem then, is there?' she said.

'Not about him, no. But what about you? Look at you! Look what you've done to yourself. "Malnutrition", that's what the doctor said. Christ! You were in a state of collapse that night: starved, half crazy, exhausted, shocked. I've never seen anything like it. And for what? Some half-baked plan to butcher a lunatic. He's a very sick man, Eileen.'

'My heart bleeds for him,' she said bitterly.

'Yeah, well it should. Mine would have done if you'd hit him with one of those bullets. Have you ever seen the results?

There's an exit hole you can put both fists into, you'd have torn him apart.'

'He wouldn't have known anything about it.'

'Oh? Just where were you going to aim?'

'At his head.'

'Really? You must be a very good shot.'

'Good enough.'

'Well, after only six months that's a little unlikely, if you'll excuse my saying so. Just suppose your aim isn't quite as good as you think. We'll leave the possibility of you hitting someone else for the moment. Suppose you hit him in the shoulder? Tear his arm right out at the socket. That be good enough? Or a leg, maybe. Or blast his guts all over the scenery. He'd know all about that, wouldn't he?'

She looked at him stonily. 'You think Hilary died painlessly?' she asked.

He stared at her incredulously. 'Oh, that's great! That's really something. Why stop at murder, Eileen? Why not kidnap him? You'll have just as much chance. Take him off to some place out of earshot and *really* make a good job of it. What's your choice, lady? Red hot pokers? Razors? Oh boy! You could gloat over him for days!'

She looked away. 'This is your little fantasy, not mine,' she said. 'Leave me out of it.'

'You don't like the idea? Okay. Who needs it? We've got fancy bullets instead. They'll do.'

'I think you're being stupid.'

'You're right. Bloody stupid. What do you think you're being?'

She remained silent. He sighed, stood up and walked across the room to her. He put his hands on her shoulders.

'Come on, honey. Look at me. This is pointless, crazy and dangerous. That's how I see it anyway. Maybe you've got a few ideas of your own. Have you? Well, if so, let's hear them. You listened to me, okay, I'll listen to you.'

'What for? Are you going to offer to do it for me?'

'Sure! You convince me, and I'll go and blast his head off if we catch him.'

She smiled, and shrugged. 'I don't know what you want me to say. Do you want a dissertation on the death penalty?'

'Okay, we'll start with that. Sit down, we'll have a debate. You're in favour, right?'

'Not necessarily.'

He looked at her blankly. Then he threw himself into a chair and ran a hand through his hair.

'Jesus! This is like arguing with an eel. You're *not* in favour of a death penalty?'

'I'm not in favour of a fixed death penalty.'

'What do you mean by that?'

'I don't think every murderer should hang.'

'Okay, I get it. Now, what about insanity?'

She looked down at him steadily. 'Let me tell you something,' she said at last. 'Out in the Far East there's a little country where the penalty for raping a child is public castration. They haven't had a case for nearly a hundred years, and they've only had one since that law was passed. A man who didn't think they'd do it. He was wrong. That proves one of two things to me. Either it's a peculiarly healthy atmosphere out there, where they don't seem to have any of these so-called psychopaths, or a violent reprisal can be a deterrent. I know which explanation I'd opt for.'

He listened carefully, and nodded when she finished.

'Well, honey,' he said, 'I don't know if you could get a law like that passed here. I doubt it, but you go ahead and try if you like. But while that particular reprisal might be a deterrent the death penalty isn't, and all the figures prove it.'

'What do the figures say about people coming out of jail and committing a second murder?'

'Okay, but this one's mad. Mentally ill.'

'Murderers who've been proved insane have been released before, and have done it again,' she said. 'Anyway, how do you know he's mad?'

'Come on! He must be!'

'Ever heard of Raymond Morris? Myra Hindley? Ian Brady? They were child killers, but they weren't mad.'

'You reckon they'll ever come out of jail?'

She shrugged. 'Maybe not. I don't know. Suppose they don't? They spend the rest of their lives in jail. What a happy prospect! At a cost of God knows how many thousands to the tax payer, which, by the way, includes me. Pretty soon I may be paying to keep the bastard who killed my daughter. To keep him fed, clothed, housed, guarded, all the little luxuries they get – and I'm expected to accept that without a murmur!'

'Okay, calm down. I can see that would rankle. But what do you suppose would happen if everybody broke the laws they personally don't like?'

'There have been a few bad laws changed that way. But the Government never takes much notice of what people want.'

'You think the majority of people want a death penalty?'

'I don't know. I don't think anybody has ever tried to find out. I think a substantial number do.'

'That's not the impression I get from what I've read.'

'The only people who write about it seem to be a bunch of arrogant pseudo-intellectuals who never think anybody else has an opinion worth listening to. You've probably talked to a lot of people while you've been on this case. What was the majority reaction there?'

'I didn't ask.'

'I bet a fair number of them volunteered an opinion, though. And I know what it would have been. They can't all be stupid or extremist or inhumane, or whatever the latest label is.'

'No, most of them are decent, kindly people, who probably haven't thought too much about it.'

'Well, *I've* thought about it.'

'You're too close to be able to judge it clearly.'

'Oh? So the very people who have been most closely affected by this sort of thing must not be heard, because of that connection?'

'That's right. You can't give a valid judgement on this, because you are personally involved. It's hard, it's unfair, but it's true.'

She looked at him coldly. 'Then there's no more to be said, is there?'

He shrugged. 'Not if you can't think of anything else to say. I've had my turn.'

She lit a cigarette, and stared down into the mews. Hardisty watched her in silence.

'When can I have my gun back?' she asked at last.

'Never.'

'You think that'll stop me?'

'I think it'll give you a problem.'

'I can get another one.'

'Not so easily. You left your permit in the car, Mrs Eileen MacNeil. Should I check up on how you got it?'

She looked at him over her shoulder. 'You're very clever, aren't you?'

'In the situation I'm in now? Come off it, baby. I'm dumb.' He smiled at her. After a moment she smiled back and walked over to the fire.

'Please can we stop talking about it now?' she asked.

'Sure. Just think about it though, will you?'

She nodded. 'Yes. I'll do that.'

He reached out a hand. 'Come here.'

She took his hand, and sat down on the arm of his chair, leaning against his shoulder, and gazing dreamily into the fire. He slid an arm round her waist and looked up at her.

'Listen,' he said. 'You ever need any help, I'm always available. Okay?'

She sighed and nodded. He reached up and pulled her head towards him.

'Poor baby,' he whispered, and kissed her gently on the lips.

She slipped down on to his lap and put her arms round him, burying her face in his shoulder.

'I wish I knew what to do. It's all so confusing.'

He stroked her hair and put his arms round her shoulders, holding her close and speaking gently.

'You've been all tied up in it for six months and you got yourself into a bad state. It'll take a while to get it back into perspective now. Don't worry, it'll come. I'll help you.'

She nodded and they sat for a long time in silence, the firelight flickering gently in the darkening room, the soft glow of the street lamps outside gleaming palely through the window.

At last she stirred.

'Dan?'

He turned his head, his lips brushing gently against her cheek, feeling her suddenly tense against him.

'Yes?'

'Dan, love me.'

His arms tightened around her convulsively as she raised her head and looked at him. Then their mouths met in a long, hungry embrace, their hands moving on each other's bodies; demanding, caressing, and they slid unknowingly to the floor, locked together in the wild urgency of their desire.

They made love many times that night, one of them wakening and turning to the other, caresses and whispers leading to the slow response, arousal and final crescendo and climax. Eileen found forgotten skills and joys returning to her under Dan's skilful hands and urgent, demanding body. At times she was roused to a wild, animal passion, and then she fought him savagely; teeth buried in his shoulder, nails raking his back, until her final joyful release, when she would fall back with a long, low cry; then awareness slowly return-ing, his long, hard body, shining with sweat, lying against her, half closed eyes watching her, his answering smile. The peaceful aftermath, sharing a cigarette, lying with her head on his shoulder, one arm flung possessively across his chest, whispering, small laughs, shared intimacies, he putting the cigarette to her lips, she tracing the line of his eyebrow, his jaw, with her finger, watching for his smile.

And then sleep, and the half-remembered strangeness of a body at her side, until she reawoke, reaching a hesitant hand across to his shoulder, listening, almost apprehensively, for the murmuring sigh that preceded his turning towards her, and the touch of his hands.

They were woken in the morning by the ringing of the telephone. Hardisty, yawning, padded through into the living room, and Eileen listened, laughing softly, to the conversa-tion.

'Hallo? ... Oh, hallo, Pat ... Yeah, she's better ... You mind your own goddamned business ... No, sweetheart, your big flat feet turn me right off ... Look, I'll be back in a couple of days, okay? ... Well, you just do that. I'll see you then.'

Eileen made breakfast in the tiny kitchen and Hardisty sat at the table watching her. While she worked she told him of what she had been doing in Brighton, carefully omitting names, until he laughed, ruffled her hair and reassured her.

'Look, honey, this old boy in the gunshop; he's done nothing wrong. Okay? Neither did the man who taught you to shoot. Far as they were concerned, you weren't breaking any laws, so you can stop being so cagey. I'm not about to go tearing up there with warrants.'

'I'd hate them to know anything about it,' she said.

'They won't. Not from me.' He looked up, and caught her doubtful glance. 'You stay away from guns and rifle ranges until all this is over and I'll make that a promise.'

She turned the bacon in the frying pan, her face troubled. Then she smiled.

'But I like shooting,' she said lightly.

'Fine,' he said, matching her tone. 'Me too. Now we've got a shared interest, so everything's wonderful.'

'I'll take you on with a rifle any day!'

'Sure. Next week, maybe.' He yawned, and she turned to look at him, smiling.

'You're still sleepy.'

'That's your fault.'

'Not entirely!'

He laughed, and reached out to catch her hand, pulling her towards him and sitting her on his lap.

'Come to sunny California,' he said, 'where we gas our murderers.'

She grimaced. 'Can I watch?'

'Sure,' he said lazily, nibbling at her ear. 'Front row seat, opera glasses and all.'

132

'Oh, goody goody!' She tried to pull herself free, and when he resisted, laughingly protested. 'Come on! The toast's burning!'

He watched her at the cooker, and saw the smile leave her face, to be replaced by a thoughtful frown.

'Was that some sort of a proposal?' she asked at last.

'Nothing so respectable. It was a proposition. Hey, come on! I'm hungry.'

She put a plate of bacon and eggs in front of him, and sat down looking at him.

'You want me to go back to America with you?' she asked at last.

'That's right.'

'Are you serious?'

He looked across the table at her, and the smile faded from his face.

'I'm serious,' he said. 'I really mean it.'

'Wow!' she said weakly.

He hid a smile, and went on eating his breakfast.

'You want me to live with you?' she asked, after a long silence.

He put down his knife and fork. 'You've been doing that for nearly a week now. What's the matter, you going down with a bad attack of morals or something?'

She made a helpless gesture. 'Oh, Dan, I don't know.'

'Well, think about it. The offer's open.'

Hardisty went out later that morning to buy a newspaper. Eileen did not hear him return, and he stood in the door of the living room watching her sadly as she attempted to pick the lock of the gun cabinet with a piece of wire. She started violently when he spoke.

'It's a five lever mortise lock,' he said. 'Case-hardened steel. And the key's in the bank, I left it there this morning.'

133

She looked at him silently. He walked across the room and put his arms around her shoulders.

'You're still determined to go on with this?' he asked quietly.

'I don't know.'

'Just remember what I said, Eileen. Just think about it.'

She nodded, and he turned away.

'Dan?'

'Yes?'

'Are you angry?'

He looked at her, smiling faintly. 'Would you mind if I were?'

'Yes.'

He sat down, and opened the newspaper. 'No, I'm not angry. I'm sorry you tried that, but I guess I should have expected it.'

She was very quiet and subdued for the rest of the morning. Finally Hardisty laughed at her, and slapped her on the bottom.

'Stupid bitch,' he said affectionately, and she smiled at him.

Later in the afternoon he set to work fixing a high shelf in the corner of the room, standing on a chair holding the screws between his teeth, the shelf resting on his shoulder. Eileen watched him for a while then wandered away, desultorily picking up magazines and newspapers, throwing them down after only a brief glance. At last, bored with the silence, she began to sing softly, looking at him sideways under lowered lashes.

> *Me no likee Blitish sailor,*
> *Yankee sailor, won't you come ashore?*

> *Me no likee Blitish sailor,*
> *Yankee sailor pay ten dollar more.*

Hardisty ignored her, concentrating on fixing a screw into a bracket. Eileen looked at him calculatingly, and went on singing, louder now.

> *Yankee sailor, he call me Sweetheart, Darling,*
> *Blitish sailor, he call me fucking whore,*
> *Yankee sailor, he . . .*

'Just a question of semantics,' said Hardisty through the screws in his teeth.

'Huh?'

He spat the screws into his hand, and turned to look at her.

'Fucking whore,' he explained succinctly. 'We use different terms. Not *sweetheart, darling.* Like I said,' he turned back to the shelf, 'it's all a question of semantics.'

'Oh,' said Eileen, blankly.

He laughed. 'Come here and hold these screws.'

After a while he looked down at her.

'You often use that sort of language?' he asked.

'Yes.'

He shook his head sorrowfully. 'Dumb, skinny and foul-mouthed,' he commented sadly. 'What the hell do I see in you?'

He drove the last screw home, jumped off the chair and smiled at her.

'Come to that, what do I see in you?' she demanded.

He held out his arms, and she stepped forward and leaned against him gratefully.

'I love you,' he said. 'You know that?'

She did not answer. After a moment he reached down and raised her head, looking down gravely into her face.

135

'I meant it.'

Still she made no reply, her face troubled and distressed. He laughed and pushed her away.

'You got no manners, that's your trouble.'

She smiled sadly, turning away. He caught her shoulder and pulled her back to face him.

'What's the matter, Eileen? Shouldn't I have said that?'

'Oh, I don't know, Dan. It's too soon, I don't know how I feel and . . .'

He put a hand across her lips, silencing her and laughed quietly. 'I'm not asking any favours, honey. No strings. I just thought I'd let you know. Okay?'

She nodded and smiled, and he hugged her briefly before letting her go. He did not mention it again.

He went back to work the following day, and Eileen stayed in the flat, busying herself with small housewifely duties, or sitting staring into the fire, thinking and dreaming, while she waited for him to return. Occasionally she looked at the gun cabinet over the desk, then her face would harden, and she lost herself again in bitter schemes and harsh memories.

In the afternoons she would go for long walks, sometimes overstressing her weakened body so that she would be forced to take a bus or a taxi home and Hardisty, returning in the evening, would see the tell-tale signs of weariness in her face, and would swear at her good-humouredly and send her to bed, while he cooked a meal and cleared it away after they had eaten.

Gradually, Eileen's strength returned and Hardisty began to relax his constant vigilance over her health, his fears for her future diminished.

Until one evening he returned from work and the green car had gone.

CHAPTER ELEVEN

'Why did she go back to Glasgow?' I asked Diane when I returned a few days later.

'I'm not sure. I think it was a bit impulsive, if you know what I mean. She was getting very fond of Dan Hardisty and I think she was subconsciously frightened of that.'

'Frightened?'

'Oh, look, I don't know, I'm not a psychiatrist. It just seems likely to me. After all, when you think of what happened to the other people she loved, it wouldn't be that surprising, would it?'

'Maybe not. You went back to see her, didn't you?'

'Yes, she telephoned me. I'd been very worried about her. I'd kept ringing the flat and there was no reply. I rang Jackie Grey and he said she'd gone north to look after a friend. I didn't know what had happened. I tried to ring Anne Butler, but she just hung up on me. Bloody bitch. So I was very relieved when I heard from her.'

'Did you notice much change in her when you went down?'

'Oh, Lord, yes! Physically, she was a different person. She'd put on about a stone in weight, she had more energy, everything. I think she'd been pretty ill when I'd seen her before. She was much fitter.'

'What about her mental state?'

'That was a different matter. Back in October she'd been holding on to this murder thing. Sort of gritted-teeth determination. I can see now that it was the only thing that kept her sane, but it was different that winter. Dan Hardisty had stepped into the picture and that clouded the issue a bit.

'Now, you may think that was a good thing, but it wasn't entirely. Being physically fitter, she was better equipped to cope with the situation, but it was much more confusing for her. She was still convinced she was right, you see, convinced this man ought to die, and Dan never really managed to convince Eileen that what she was doing was wrong. He talked to her, listened to her, argued with her – everything he could, to do him justice – but she never became convinced that it was wrong for her to go out and kill him. All he had done was show her what would happen if she succeeded, and I gather he painted a pretty grim picture. She'd never looked that far ahead until then. And, of course, he'd shown her an alternative. But all it had really done was confuse her. She'd had this idea for a long time and it wasn't going to be that easy to forget it all. He knew that, of course, he knew it would take time, but that was just what she wouldn't give him. Maybe she knew it too, felt her resolve weakening, so she just cut out quick.'

I shook my head.

'I'm sorry, Diane,' I said, 'but I'm finding this very hard to understand. After a whole month of argument and persuasion, she *still* felt just as determined?'

'I don't know how she *felt*,' retorted Diane. 'She told *me* she didn't love him and wouldn't go away with him anyway, and she told *me* she was just as determined. What the hell do you expect me to do? I'm not a mind reader. And anyway, no handsome yankee copper had come into my life. I hadn't forgotten how Janice died.'

I kept my thoughts to myself on that, and after a moment Diane shrugged, and resumed.

'Well, you think what you like. I can only tell you what

138

happened. She still wouldn't hear of me doing it, even though I offered, so don't blame me.

'So then we had the problem of getting another gun. Eileen didn't dare try and get a replacement for the permit she'd lost, they can be very difficult about that and they'd have been bound to make enquiries. She didn't want to go back and work for Jackie Grey either, even though I thought it was the answer. What she said she'd do was go back to the night club where she'd worked before her marriage, and try to get one through some people she might meet there. It wasn't exactly a criminal dive, I don't think, but there were probably a few fringe elements there. She said it was the best she could do. It was a bit unsatisfactory, but there it was. Apart from that we were to carry on as before.'

'This idea, it's all a bit vague, isn't it? Getting a gun illegally from some people she might meet, but she didn't know who. Didn't it occur to you then that maybe she didn't want to succeed?'

'No, it didn't. She said she wanted to go ahead.'

'Did you have to persuade her?'

'No, I did not. It was her idea in the first place, remember? She said she would go ahead.' Diane was staring at me defiantly.

I shrugged. 'All right. You went back to London after that, did you?'

'That's right. I didn't see her again until it was all over, and you know everything else I had to do with it. I don't think I can help you any more.'

Shortly after that I left. I did not see Diane again. She had helped me a lot, and I think she had been genuinely fond of Eileen Denham, but for all that I can only remember her as an embittered woman who deliberately exploited the mental confusion of her friend for her own violent ends. Had she

139

not been so determined on revenge, had she not deliberately turned a blind eye to Eileen's increasing doubts, the resulting tragedy might never have taken place.

Eileen, Sweetheart,

Do you know I sat here for nearly five minutes trying to think of a way to start this letter? What shall I call you, dear Sir or Madam? Well, there it is, 'Eileen, Sweetheart', and now I'll chew my pen for another five minutes while I think of a way to go on.

Why did you go? Were you unhappy here? Did I do or say something that made you want to leave? I didn't mean to.

I love you. Now you've got it on paper, black and white, so I'm caught! What will you do with me? It doesn't matter how you feel about me. What does matter — what is far, far more important — is that you are not well, and I am worried about you.

If you want to come back, just walk in, you have a key. It's your home if you want it.

Whatever happens, I'm here if you need me. Whistle, and I'll come running!

Take care of yourself, Eileen.
I love you.
Dan.

My dear Dan,

Thank you for your letter. Like you, I had trouble starting mine.

I am sorry I had to go like that, but I want to be on my own for a while. I hope you can understand. Please don't worry about me, I am all right.

I am bad at writing letters, so forgive me for a short note.

I am sorry, Dan, but I don't want to go to America.
                         Love from
                            Eileen.

Hallo, Smiler!
   *Thanks for the letter – all packed with news and views and
higher thoughts as it was.*
   *How are you, Skinny? Back on a starvation plan or getting
a middle-aged spread? Let me know, and I'll send you a loaf of
bread or a diet sheet, whichever you need.*
   *So you don't want to go to 'America'. Well, okay, who needs
'America'? How about Greenland?*
                         I love you.
                            Dan.

My dear Dan,
   *Thank you for your letter. I am quite well, and I am eating
enough, but I am not fat, so you can keep your loaf of bread
and your diet sheet.*
   *I don't want to go to Greenland either. Are you crazy? I like
it where I am.*
                        Love from
                           Eileen.

Glasgow in January: the snow came late that year and
Hogmanay was past before the pale clouds rolled in, and the
first lazy flakes began to fall, settling silently on the black roofs
or touching briefly on the wet roads before twinkling into
oblivion.

Faster and faster the white flakes fell, hypnotic in their
silent whirl, obscuring the harsh outlines of the black buildings, softening stark silhouettes, piling in hard-packed heaps
on the sides of the pavements where the traffic constantly

hissed and sprayed along the salted roads, headlights gleaming on the wet black surface.

The city was transformed, sounds muffled by the dense white covering, the skyline a splendid Arctic vision, white snow and blue ice against the black mass of the distant hills.

Eileen would return from work just before dawn, booted feet sliding through the snow that returned every night, head bowed against the cold wind, hands thrust deep into the pockets of her coat. She slept through the days, rising in the late afternoon to face the prospect of work that night with a feeling of grey weariness that had nothing to do with physical fatigue.

At the club, against the background of muted lights and laughter, she behaved with gay insouciance, brittle amusement lighting her face, a thin veneer of charm masking her near desperation.

Eileen, Sweetheart,

    You are a lousy letter writer. Grab a telephone, will you?

    What are you doing with yourself these days? Give me a call and let me know what's going on.

                I love you.

                 Dan.

Robin Adair, a romantically named man with the thin, ascetic face of a monk, the dreamy manner of a mystic and the mind and profession of a criminal; a confidence trickster, swindler, and occasional burglar, his visits to the club were regarded with suspicion and dislike by the two owners who suspected, probably rightly, that his companions were all too often intended victims, brought there for some purpose they could not understand.

They warned Eileen about him the first time he called in, and she looked across the room at him with interest.

'He's a *stinker*!' whispered Derek dramatically, affectedly twirling his cigarette in its amber holder. 'Don't have anything to do with him, darling, not a *thing*!'

'He's right, you know,' said Matt, leaning towards her confidentially. 'What's more, he *never* has any money. I wish he'd stay away. *Beastly* little man.'

'Why do you suppose he comes here?' asked Eileen.

'We prefer not to know,' sniffed Derek.

'Does he come often?'

'Far *too* often.'

Eileen smiled, and moved away.

Adair returned two weeks later, and Eileen waited until his companion went up to the bar before she approached his table.

'Mr Adair?'

He looked up slowly, and regarded her with faint surprise.

'I need help. Can you come to this address tomorrow afternoon?' She held out a slip of paper.

He continued to look at her.

'There's money in it,' she added.

He smiled faintly, and took the paper from her hand.

'Of course,' he said quietly, and turned his head away.

He arrived early the following afternoon and sat on the sofa looking at her with an air of polite enquiry.

'Can I pour you a drink?' she asked.

'Thank you, no.'

She sat down opposite him and lit a cigarette.

'I need a gun,' she said quickly. 'A rifle.'

His thin lips twitched with faint distaste. 'I think you have come to the wrong man,' he replied, speaking slowly and distantly, enunciating every syllable with careful clarity. 'I do not have anything to do with firearms.'

'I realise that. I'm in a difficult position, Mr Adair. Surely

143

you have some contacts who might help me?'

He nodded, smiling faintly. 'I may be able to help you. You realise that this will be expensive?'

'Yes.'

'My own services in this matter will not be cheap. I will require fifty pounds now, and a further fifty pounds when I have supplied you with a name and an address.'

She reached for her handbag. 'Will you take a cheque?'

'I would prefer cash.'

He watched her counting out the money, and then leaned forward and spoke again.

'Please listen carefully and remember what I say. The next time that I come into the club I will be alone. I will sit at the bar and I will wait until you are serving the drinks. I will ask for a whisky and I will hand you a one pound note in payment. That one pound note will be folded in half, inside it will be a slip of paper on which I will have printed a name and an address. You will be able to obtain what you require there, but the terms of your purchase will be no concern of mine. The rifle will be given to you with some vital part of its mechanism missing. When you have paid a further fifty pounds into my account, in cash without using your own name, that part of the mechanism will be sent to you by post. These precautions may sound melodramatic, but I am still in business only because I take melodramatic precautions.'

Eileen nodded, and handed over the money. 'Thank you. I'll remember.'

He stood up. 'Please do not attempt to contact me. It will take me about two weeks to make the necessary arrangements. The name and address of my bank and my account number, will be on the paper I will give you. Thank you, I will see myself out.'

* * *

144

In the Midlands, the huge machine that had been set up in the early part of the previous summer was slowly grinding to a halt. A skeleton staff was still maintained at the information centre, a clerk at the almost silent switchboard, another at the massive banks of filing cabinets, but most of the men who had been closely involved in one of the biggest manhunts in the history of the British police force had returned to routine duties, and the men who had led it were faced, inevitably, with the bitter prospect of failure.

Life in Hallerton had returned to normal. The few posters with the pictures of the murdered children and the photograph of the green car that still remained on the walls and billboards were tattered and streaked with grime. There were children playing in the streets again and it had been many months since a road block had been set up in a fast, intensive search for a missing child.

Walshe gave a brief press conference to explain the impending return of the three men to London, and the scant attention the reports received in the papers underlined the dwindling interest of the public in the crimes that had been committed in the previous summer. His assurances that they would return to Hallerton, that the case was by no means closed, were not even mentioned in many of the articles. His bitterness increased and he became taciturn and short-tempered.

The unfortunate Palmer, smarting under a stinging and hardly deserved retort in answer to an innocent question, took refuge in Hardisty's office, and voiced his grievances loudly and emphatically to the laconic American, who continued writing under the barrage of embittered verbiage that was hurled at his head.

'Christ, it's not my fault we didn't catch the bastard! I worked like a bloody slave, sweated blood, did everything, but

145

everything, he wanted. The overtime I've put in on this, it's unbelievable, and what do I get?'

'Paid,' commented Hardisty, turning over a page.

'Aren't you the clever one? Well, okay, you tell me what I'm supposed to do. The whole damned office cluttered up with those bloody files, and all I asked...'

'Yeah, I know, I heard you. And Bill Walshe was unsympathetic. What do you want me to do?'

'*Unsympathetic!* That's the bloody understatement of the year. If he'd said that on the factory floor there'd have been a strike. Who the hell does he think he is?'

'He's the boss, that's who he thinks he is. Console yourself, Pat, in two days' time we'll all be gone.'

'I can't wait. What happens then, Dan? You going back to California?'

'Yeah, pretty soon I guess. I'll hang on here for a while. I'm due for some leave, I'll take that before I go.'

Palmer stood up. 'Going up to Glasgow to see the fair Eileen?'

Hardisty smiled sardonically. 'I seem to have said this before Pat, you mind your own goddamned business.'

Walshe grunted sourly when Hardisty brought up the question of leave.

'How long do you want?'

'Three weeks?'

'Hm. Yes. Yes, I think that can be arranged.' He smiled wryly. 'Maybe our tempers will have healed by then. What are your plans after that?'

Hardisty sat on a corner of Walshe's desk, lit a cigarette and blew a plume of smoke thoughtfully towards the window.

'I'm not sure, Bill. I was told I could see this case out.'

Walshe grunted again. 'I see your problem. That fella who

146

came with you, what was his name? Hughes? He's already gone, hasn't he?'

Hardisty nodded.

'We're not beaten yet, you know,' said Walshe aggressively.

'I know that, Bill. That's not what's bothering me. It's just how long I can wait for it to break.'

'How much leeway do you think they'll give you?'

'I don't know. I may get called back right away, or they may leave it for another couple of months. They're not exactly overstaffed over there.'

'Suppose I were to tell the Assistant Commissioner I needed you?'

Hardisty grinned, and stood up.

'Then it'd be up to your boss and mine, wouldn't it? I don't know about yours, but mine can be a cussed old bastard.'

Walshe smiled. 'How do you feel about it?' he asked. 'Do you want to stay on for a while?'

'Yeah, I'd like to see this one out. I'm in no hurry to go back, it's been a terrific experience working over here.'

'Well, I'll see what I can do, then.'

The snow was thawing fast, an unseasonal warm spell crossing the country, bringing in its wake high winds and heavy rainfall. The storm damage was bad, even for a country used to gale force winds, huge tracts of forests torn and flattened, low lying areas flooded, and buildings left roofless, or with windows and doors torn loose.

Glasgow was badly hit. A huge crane on the dockside had torn free from its restraining chains, the jib had buckled and swung into the side of a warehouse, tearing down half the wall, before the entire crane had collapsed onto the dockside, killing a fireman and injuring several people in its path. A tug had slipped its moorings and drifted into a group of boats moored in midstream, sinking two and causing considerable damage to the remainder. A block of flats had begun to crack, and had been hastily evacuated and shored up to await more seasonal weather, when a detailed inspection could be made to decide its fate.

Eileen, following her meeting with Robin Adair, was in a tense, nervous condition, alternating quickly between bouts of the uttermost depression (when she would lie on her bed throughout the days staring at the ceiling, often contemplating suicide) and wild, exhausting spells of exaggerated emotion, laughing almost hysterically at the mildest joke, or furiously angry at an imagined insult. At these times she would spend hours in her flat, crying with self-pity and despising herself bitterly as she did so.

She telephoned Diane Clayton the day after she had seen Robin Adair, and told her what had been arranged. Diane congratulated her on her luck. Eileen hung up after the conversation and abandoned herself to a long bout of tears.

She was in a mood of high elation when Hardisty rang the bell of her flat, a mood engendered by nothing more than the purchase of a dress for her work at the club which she felt suited her. She was standing in front of the mirror, turning this way and that, looking over her shoulder, twisting her hair over her head, trying different poses.

She started violently when the bell rang and stood for a moment, her eyes closed, feeling her heart thudding erratically. Then she shook her head in irritation at herself and walked through the hall to the front door.

'Hi there,' said Dan stepping past her and smiling down at her.

It was only after I had interviewed several different people, and heard many, sometimes conflicting, stories, that I managed to deduce what had happened when Dan Hardisty arrived at Eileen's flat late that evening.

It appears that he asked her to spend his leave with him and she, thinking of her future appointment with Robin Adair, made some excuse and refused to do so. An argument had developed during the course of which Eileen, probably in one of the fits of uncontrollable rage to which she was subject, had either directly told Hardisty that she intended to obtain another gun, or else sufficiently roused his suspicions for him to take the course of action he chose. Since I cannot imagine how, if the former were the case, she had prevented him from immediately going to the police and telling them the whole story, I am inclined to believe that it was her attitude to him and her general frame of mind, that caused him to suspect her intentions.

Whatever happened at that meeting, Hardisty left some two hours later, and the following day hired a Ford Mustang, a car with a sufficient turn of speed to deal with Eileen's Jaguar, and spent some days following her. He even spent the nights sleeping in the car parked outside the block of flats.

Naturally, Eileen did not accept this situation with anything approaching equanimity. There were several quarrels, and a painful scene in the club was only averted when Hardisty paid a large sum of money to one of the owners, who promptly told Eileen to take the choice between accepting his presence with a good grace or finding herself another job. To do the man justice, he and his partner had been regretting their offer of a job to Eileen; they were concerned about her, but they were rather more concerned about the effect her strange behaviour was having on their customers. Eileen eventually appeared to become resigned to the situation, and even made the best of it by allowing Hardisty to drive her to and from work. However, they parted at the door of her home, she went to her flat, and he gained what sleep he could behind the wheel of the car.

It was approximately a week after Hardisty's arrival in Glasgow that Robin Adair came into the club. Eileen was serving behind the bar at the time and she spotted him immediately as he walked down the stairs. She glanced quickly at Hardisty, who was sitting at his usual place at the bar, staring down into a glass of whisky. He looked up at her, and she turned away quickly, busying herself among the glasses.

She turned back as Adair leaned across the polished counter, and approached him, a fixed smile of welcome on her face.

'Can I help you, sir?'

Even to her own ears her voice sounded elaborately casual and she noticed with a mixture of alarm and irritation that Hardisty had raised his head and was looking at her curiously.

'I'll have a Grouse please.'

She went back to the racks and reached for a glass, looking quickly in the mirror at Hardisty as she did so. He was frowning at her thoughtfully, and as she watched he turned his head to study Adair carefully.

She poured the whisky and took it back to him, sliding it across the bar towards him. The folded pound note changed hands. Adair looked round slowly and met Hardisty's stare.

Eileen walked back to the till and slid the pound note under the wire catch in the tray, her eyes on the mirror. Hardisty was frowning down into his glass again, his fingers drumming slowly on the bar.

150

Quickly, she slipped her fingers under the note and grasped the slip of paper there. Watching him carefully, she slid it under her cuff.

Adair was looking at her out of the corner of his eye. As she turned away from the till he looked back at Hardisty, his eyes narrowed thoughtfully. Eileen hesitated, glancing from one to the other, struggling to control her rising panic. She had never before encountered such an aura of tension as that which surrounded the two men: Adair rigid and motionless, hardly seeming to breathe; Hardisty still drumming his fingers on the polished wood of the bar, not raising his eyes, but obviously intensely aware both of her and of the man standing a few feet away from him.

She turned decisively and walked away. Adair did not move, but Hardisty glanced up quickly as she stepped through the door of the office, and when he looked down away the frown was deeper than before. Slowly, he turned his head towards Adair.

Some minutes passed. Then Adair raised his glass, finished the whisky, and turned to leave. Hardisty immediately rose to his feet and strode over to the door through which Eileen had vanished. He threw it open, immediately saw the open window leading into the little courtyard and turned back into the room.

Adair had not seemed to hurry, but he had reached the top of the stairs before Hardisty closed the door. A quick glance over his shoulder ascertained that the tall American was striding across the room towards the foot of the stairs. Adair walked quickly through the small hallway and out into the street towards the little alley down which he could escape.

Hardisty bounded up the stairs, shouldered past a couple in the hall and swung through the door on to the pavement, looking to right and left for Adair. He saw him hurrying down the road, and set off in pursuit, weaving through the small knot of people outside the club.

Adair looked round and saw Hardisty striding down the pavement after him. At once he broke into a run, reached the entrance of the alley in a few steps and turned into it, where he sprinted for the other end and the comparative safety of the late night crowds in the busy street into which it led.

Cursing, Hardisty raced after him and skidded into the alley behind him, crashing against the wall on the far side as he did so. The slight figure running from him was closer now and Hardisty threw himself forward, his long legs eating up the ground as the distance between them narrowed.

Adair panicked as he heard the pounding footsteps behind him draw closer. Instinctively and desperately, he glanced up and ahead.

The brick wall to his side was perhaps eight feet high, smooth and unbroken for many yards. He glanced over his shoulder as Hardisty reached forward to grab him. Frantically he swerved and leapt for the wall.

Hardisty, taken by surprise, overshot him and skidded to a halt, crashing down on to one knee as he tried to stop and swearing wildly at the pain. He spun back fast and leapt for the wall as Adair straddled it, shifting his grip to take his weight as he swung himself over.

Hardisty's hand reached his ankle and he looked down to see the tall man brace himself against the wall, both hands now gripped firmly round his foot and twisting savagely. Adair screamed with pain and swung his other foot back, lashing out desperately. His heel caught Hardisty over the eye and the grip loosened fractionally. Frantically, Adair twisted, and as his foot came free he jack-knifed back to the wall, his injured foot slammed against it, instinctively scrabbling for a toe-hold.

A wave of nausea from the pain swept over him. He clung desperately to the wall, his hands slipping helplessly, as Hardisty regained his feet and launched himself at the wall again, reaching unerringly for the injured leg.

Adair screamed again as Hardisty threw himself back from the wall, and this time the smaller man was helpless against the vicious onslaught and crashed back on to the footpath, rolling away and tearing free from the murderously powerful fingers that had been locked around his foot.

Hardisty reached Adair again as he tried to stand and as they fell to the ground yet again he drove his elbow savagely down into Adair's stomach.

Adair screamed hoarsely at the sudden agony, but Hardisty's hands reached round his throat cutting off his breath, choking him as he clawed weakly and helpless at the locked fingers.

'Where has she gone?' Hardisty's voice hissed in his ear. Momentarily, the fingers loosened, and Adair's breath came in rasping heaves as he twisted wildly. Hardisty's fist crashed against the side of his head, slamming his face into the wall and tearing the skin from his cheek and jaw. As he shook his head in agony the hands gripped his throat again.

'Has she gone after a gun?'

There was a roaring in his ears and his sight was failing, and then Hardisty relaxed his grip again.

'Yes.'

'*Where?*'

Wildly, Adair lashed out at the face looming over him, the heel of his hand striking hard on the cheekbone. Hardisty swore and swung his open hand hard against Adair's bleeding face. Retching uncontrollably, Adair turned his head, reaching up to protect his face with his hands.

'*Where?*'

'Rutherglen. John Street.' The voice was a choking sob.

Hardisty stood up slowly, and stared down at the man huddled on the ground. Then he turned on his heel and strode back down the alley.

Adair twisted towards the wall, drawing up his knees as the first waves of unconsciousness rolled over him. His last memory before he finally blacked out was the bitter taste of his own vomit in his mouth.

A heavy mist was rolling off the Clyde and swirling in thick yellow coils around the street lamps as Hardisty parked the Mustang at the end of the road. He glanced at his watch quickly, and then stared down the street, gnawing his lip as he calculated the time it would take Eileen to reach him.

He smoked a cigarette, eyes and ears strained to catch a sight or sound of her, and then he got out of the car, locked it and began to walk slowly down the pavement, rubber soled shoes squeaking faintly on the wet surface.

He was half-way down the road when the sound of hurrying footsteps reached his ears, a quick tattoo of high-heeled shoes following him along the pavement. He glanced over his shoulder, but the mist hid everything more than a few yards away. Quickly, he stepped into a shop doorway and pressed into the corner, hidden in the dark shadows.

Eileen hurried past him, head bowed against the fine rain that misted her hair, hands thrust deep into the pockets of her coat. A few yards further on she slowed down and stopped under the street lamp. She looked around her, listening carefully, and then walked towards a door, peering closely through the gloom at the number painted on it.

She stepped back from the door, glanced up and down the street again and began to retrace her steps. Hardisty watched her as she hesitated, looking towards a lighted window on the other side of the road. She stood for a moment, and then she turned abruptly and looked straight into the doorway in which he hid. He saw a flicker of uncertainty cross her face, and as she narrowed her eyes and looked more closely he shrugged and stepped out into the light.

She stared at him blankly. Then she noticed the deep graze on his forehead and her face hardened in anger.

'What did you do to him?'

'Nothing he wouldn't have done to me if he'd been big enough.'

She drew in a deep breath. 'You sound like some character out of a cheap gangster novel. I suppose I'm meant to be impressed by that. Well, I'm not, Dan, I'm just disgusted.'

'I'm very sorry about that.' His voice was heavy with sarcasm. 'Naturally, I'm all burned up about the way you feel. If I'd realised it was going to upset you I wouldn't have done it.'

'And what are you going to do now?'

He leaned back against the wall and folded his arms. 'My God, am I tired of that question,' he said quietly. 'What am I going to do now? I don't know Eileen, I really don't know. How the hell did I ever get into this mess? Jesus! A year ago, if somebody had told me I'd be in this position I'd have said they were crazy. Now I'm beginning to wonder if I am.'

'Yes, you are in a mess now, aren't you?' she agreed. 'Apart from the way you look,' she added as he raised a hand to his forehead. 'I'm talking about assault. Maybe, what is it they call it? Grievous bodily harm? Is that the right term?'

'I doubt if he'll bring charges.'

'Oh, I'm sure he won't. But it hasn't actually strengthened your position, has it? Quite apart from what it's done to my opinion of you.'

Abruptly, she turned away and walked down the road. He pushed himself away from the wall and slowly walked after her. She hesitated and stopped.

'Are you going to follow me all night?'

'If I have to.'

She stood in silence for a few moments, staring down at the ground where the yellow lamplight gleamed on the wet black surface. Then she raised her head and looked at him.

'Yes, Dan, I think you're going to have to.'

CHAPTER TWELVE

It was from Bill Walshe himself that I learned about the episodes that followed Hardisty's somewhat dramatic re-entry into the story. Dick Farley, who had kept in touch with him since the case was closed, had telephoned him when he returned from Germany, and had mentioned my visit. When I returned to my flat after my abortive trip to the United States I found a letter from him in which he said that Farley had told him I wanted to talk to him and inviting me to call on him at his home one evening.

I thanked him for his invitation when I arrived at the little semi-detached house in which he lived. He shrugged, and smiled.

'Oh, well. It'll save me writing it. You know. In my memoirs. When I retire.'

'Are you going to do that?'

'I don't know. Obligatory, isn't it? Now I can copy it. From your book.'

It was early in the evening when I arrived, and we talked into the small hours of the morning. For the first two hours or so he told me of the police work that had been done, the details of the investigation, much of which I had already learned from Farley and Palmer. Then I turned my questions towards Dan Hardisty.

'He must have been mad,' said Walshe emphatically.

'Bloody crackers. He got infatuated with that crazy woman. You know. Anything to protect her. And where did it get him? Or her?'

'What should he have done?'

'Come and told me about it, of course.'

'I thought he did.'

'Oh, yes. The first time. When she took his gun. Bit worrying, that, but not much to be done about it. Never really thought much more about it. But the second time! You know, when she went after that fella on the moor. No excuse for not telling me then.'

'Didn't Pat Palmer know about that?'

'He knew she was there. Knew about the hit and run driver, of course. Never connected the two. Well, who would? None of his business who Dan Hardisty had in his flat.'

'No, I see. But what would have happened to Eileen Denham if you had been told about it?'

Walshe shrugged, and leaned back in his chair.

'Hard to say now. We'd have charged her. Couldn't have done anything else, not that time. She'd almost certainly have been sent to a psychiatric hospital. Best place for her. Might have got her straightened out then. Doubt if they'll ever do it now. She's in a mess.'

'You're right of course and I agree with you, but this is hindsight, isn't it? I'm trying to see what motivated Dan Hardisty at the time.'

'God knows!' Walshe exploded. 'Just got in deeper and deeper. Bloody fool. Wanted her to go back to America with him. Thought he could persuade her to give up. Talked 'til he was black in the face.'

'But if he'd succeeded, that would have been the best answer, wouldn't it?'

'He couldn't succeed. Never could have persuaded her.

Psychiatrist said that in court. She had an obsession. She couldn't help it, poor woman.'

He leaned forward and pointed his pipe at me. 'Look,' he said, 'I'm not much good at this psychiatric business. I'm just a simple copper, I catch the buggers and let other people sort them out later. But even I could have seen this. She couldn't give up. Even if she wanted to, which she probably did. We hadn't caught him. Dan Hardisty said we wouldn't ever catch him. Said it to her, anyway. Never said it to me. What happened? She probably believed him. What did she do? Went and got a gun anyway. Nobody to use it on. But she couldn't help herself. Jumping Jehoshaphat, my half-witted mother-in-law could have seen she was cracked!'

'Did he know she'd been mentally ill before?'

'Damned well should have done. Two and two still make four. She told him she'd been ill after her husband died. What did he think she'd had, piles? I'm sorry, I shouldn't have said that,' he apologised quickly. 'Just gets me blazing mad when I think about it.'

'Oh, that's all right. Look, I don't know a great deal about psychiatry either. But to look at the other side of the story, if you were really close to someone, don't you think it might be more difficult to tell?'

'Maybe. I don't know. At first, I suppose it would. But later? He must have realised. He wasn't a half wit.'

I nodded, and waited for him to go on. After a minute he did so.

'I liked Dan. Got on well with him. You know. He was a great help to us. Damned good policeman. That made it worse.'

'When you went back to London he went up to Glasgow, right? What happened when he was up there?'

'Ah, yes. Started off by having a row with her. Stormed

out of the flat. Don't know what it was about, pack of bloody lies he told me afterwards, wouldn't fool anybody. Went off and hired a Ford Mustang. Followed her around. You knew all that?'

'Not in any detail. Just take it that I only know what came out in court, would you?'

'Okay. One thing, though. Official Secrets Act. You know. Have to be a bit careful.'

'I understand.'

'Right. Well, he saw this character at the night club where she worked. Okay? Smelt something fishy. The girl skipped out. So he followed the character. Somehow...' he paused, and pursed his lips thoughtfully. '*Persuaded*, yes, that's the right word, persuaded him to say where she'd gone. Don't know this officially, mind you. Wasn't anything to do with me.'

'Just conjecture?'

'That's it,' he agreed. 'Conjecture. Educated guesswork, if you like. Not the way a policeman works. Facts and deduction, that's the way we do it.

'May I be forgiven,' he added unexpectedly, raising his eyes to the ceiling.

I laughed. 'However you do it, in this case you didn't?'

'Right. None of my business. Like I said. Up to the Glasgow lot if they want to dig it up. Which they don't.'

'So, where were we? Character gave him an address. Name of a road, anyway. Off goes Dan and meets her there. What happens? Another bloody row. What did he expect? So she storms off and he follows. Trails her all round Glasgow. What a pantomime, I ask you! Winds up in one of the rough areas, you know. Well, even if you don't she certainly did. She had friends down there, and she went to see them. Left him out on the pavement outside wandering

160

around like a spare ... Well, wandering around anyway. They made a couple of 'phone calls. Maybe. Like you said, it's conjecture.

'Anyway, however it happened, when she came out again she tried to make him give up following her. He wouldn't. What happened? He got beaten up.'

'By her friends.'

Walshe looked at me quizzically. 'I don't know,' he said deliberately. 'Maybe just coincidence. But let's conject a bit further, if that's the right verb. Let's say by her friends. Or her friends' friends. Do you know what they did to him?'

'I only know he got beaten up.'

'Wrong word. Carved up, more like it. Didn't get those scars on his face from a fist.'

'Razors?'

'Probably. It's been known. Brass knuckles, too. And a boot in the head.'

'Was he badly hurt?'

'Badly enough. Got back to her place in a taxi. She took him in. Nursed him back to health.'

'But she'd set it up?'

'Had she? I don't know. Don't think she thought they'd do that, even if she did. Which I never said.'

'Conjecture,' I agreed.

He nodded. 'Lovely word, that. Conjecture.'

Eileen had been back at her flat for just over an hour when the doorbell rang. She jumped, startled, and looked at her watch. It was half past three in the morning.

She had hidden the gun under a loose floorboard in her bedroom and was about to nail the board back in place when the ring on the doorbell interrupted her. Slowly she rose to her feet and kicked the hammer under the bed.

The bell rang again, shrill and demanding, and she pulled the rug back over the floor and ran to the door.

Hardisty was leaning against the frame, one hand pressed against the bell, his head resting on his arm. As Eileen opened the door he staggered and she caught him as he lurched forward, her knees sagging at the unexpected weight. Frantically, she tried to push him upright, but he was too heavy for her, and as he fell to the floor she dropped to her knees beside him, staring down in horror at the blood seeping through the torn cloth of his coat. Slowly and painfully he pushed himself off the floor and turned towards her. She gasped as she saw his face, then his eyelids flickered and he fell back unconscious.

Eileen stood up and closed the door. She looked down at him indecisively, bent down and tried to lift him. He groaned, and she straightened up, tears of fright and frustration stinging her eyes, and ran a hand through her hair in a gesture of despair.

Her hand was sticky with blood and she looked at it with a shudder of disgust. She drew a deep breath and stepped round behind his head. Gritting her teeth, she stooped and grasped him firmly under the arms. She pulled as hard as she could and he slid a few inches along the floor. Determinedly, she tugged again, and he half opened his eyes and muttered something indistinguishable.

'Dan!'

He sighed and turned his head away, his eyes closing again.

'Oh, Dan, wake up, please wake up!'

She reached forward and grasped him again, heaving him back towards her.

He caught his breath in a sharp hiss of pain and his eyes flashed open again.

'Dan?'

He stared at her blankly, raising a hand to the ragged edges of raw flesh along his jaw.

'Dan, please say something!'

'What?'

She looked around frantically as though searching for help and then clenched her fists in an effort to bring herself under control.

'Look, can you get up?'

He looked at her, and shook his head as though trying to clear it, wincing with the pain.

'Oh, damn it, get up!' she yelled.

He flinched and painfully raised himself up on one elbow. She stooped and reached for his arm.

'Come *on*! You can't stay there!'

'Oh, shut up.'

'Please, Dan, get up!'

'Okay, just give me a minute, will you?'

He turned his head and looked down at his blood-soaked sleeve. 'Ah, bloody hell!'

'What happened?'

He looked up at her cynically. 'Don't tell me you don't know.'

Eileen bit her lip. 'I never dreamed they'd do anything like this,' she whispered.

Hardisty laughed shortly, and a spasm of pain crossed his face. Eileen knelt down beside him.

'I'd better call an ambulance, hadn't I?'

'No.'

'Why not?'

'Because they'd ask a lot of awkward questions.'

She sat back and looked at him despairingly. 'But what am I to do then?'

He looked at her thoughtfully. Then he slowly sat up and reached out a hand. 'Pull me up.'

Eileen took his arm, stood up and pulled him to his feet. For a moment he swayed and reached out for the wall to steady himself, his face contorted with pain. Eileen stepped forward and put an arm round his waist, pulling his arm over her shoulder.

'Come on, let's get you to bed.'

He grunted, and leaned against her as she turned towards the bedroom door. Slowly and painfully they crossed the hall. At the door he stopped and leaned against the frame.

'Hold on a minute.'

Eileen looked up at him. His face was ashen, the cuts and bruises livid against the pallor of his skin. Sweat stood out on his forehead and his eyes were closed.

'Oh, Dan, for God's sake let me call an ambulance!'

He shook his head slowly and pushed himself upright. He staggered the last few steps and collapsed on to the bed, his jaw clenched, his breath coming in short gasps.

Eileen sat on the bed beside him and stared down at his battered face.

'Dan?'

His eyelids flickered briefly, then he sighed and his body went limp.

When he opened his eyes again Eileen had removed his coat and shoes. The tattered fragments of his shirt, which she had cut away, were lying in a bloodstained heap on the floor. His right arm and hand were bandaged with strips she had torn from a sheet and she was bathing the cuts on his forehead from a bowl of water standing on the table beside the bed. He turned his head slowly and looked at the bandages on his arm.

'Does it feel better?' she asked.

'Feels different anyway,' he replied cautiously.

She smiled tremulously, wrung out the pad of cotton wool and swabbed tentatively at the gash over his eyebrow. He winced, but made no sound until she reached the jaw, where the brass knuckle duster had torn open the flesh, leaving it bruised and ragged, an ugly split along the line of the bone. As she dabbed the swab at the broken flesh he gasped and caught her hand, the sweat springing out on his forehead.

Eileen sobbed and looked away, brushing the tears out of her eyes with an angry gesture. After a moment she turned back and looked down at him.

'Dan, *please* let me call an ambulance.'

'No.' He had thrown his left arm across his eyes, and he spoke through clenched teeth.

'Look, I can't cope with this! Don't you understand? You're badly hurt, I don't know what to do!'

'You're doing fine.'

'Suppose that goes septic?'

'It won't.'

Eileen turned away angrily. 'You're always so damned sure, aren't you? Why couldn't you stay out of this? It's your own fault if you get roughed up.'

He winced. 'I wish you'd stop shouting.'

'Oh, I'm sorry.'

He did not answer. After a moment he closed his eyes again and leaned his head back.

'Did you get the gun?' he asked eventually.

'What does it matter?'

'Did you?'

'Yes.'

He sighed, and turned away from her. She stayed looking down at him for a while, then walked away and stood staring out of the window across the grey roofs of the town where the first light of dawn was streaking the eastern sky and glinting on the wet tiles.

He was silent for so long that she thought he had fallen asleep, and she jumped when he spoke to her.

'I've been wondering how I'd react if somebody killed Terry,' he said. 'I suppose if I caught up with him right away I might kill him. But months later? And planning all the way? I don't know. Do you think you could explain it to me?'

She looked across the room at him and slowly walked over to the bed, clasping and unclasping her hands as she sought for the words. He smiled up at her as she sat down beside him. She threw back her head, frowned for a moment and began to speak.

'After Robin died I was ill. I don't remember much about it. He'd been dying for months, it was almost a relief when it was over. I just gave up.'

She bit her lip and looked away towards the window again. For a long time she was silent.

'While I was ill,' she went on eventually, 'Hilary was in a home. I haven't any relatives and the only ones Robin had were in South Africa. There wasn't anywhere else for her to go.'

She frowned again and looked down at her hands clasped in her lap.

'When I got better,' she said slowly, 'I went to collect Hilary to bring her home.'

She stopped, the picture of the child as she had been then suddenly vivid in her mind. Huge dark eyes in the pale face; quiet, grave, composed; black hair drawn back tidily in an alice band, standing beside a suitcase in the dark, marble-floored hall, her new green coat and tan gloves very smart and clean, the kindly matron stooping to place a quick, motherly kiss on the cool little face.

Eileen winced as she recalled the mute appeal for help in the child's eyes as she looked up at the old nurse, and the quiet resignation in her face as she turned back to this strange woman who was her mother.

'I'd let her down, you see,' she whispered. 'I thought because Robin was dead it was all over and I could let go.'

Little Hilary, the dark, elfin child plunged terrifyingly into the adult world of grief and death. To whom could she turn?

'I forgot about Hilary.'

Surrounded by strangers, her big, laughing father incomprehensibly 'dead', her mother 'not well, darling, but she'll be back soon'. Soon. Months later, when the kindly strangers had soothed her grief, reassured her fears and given her the security for which she had so desperately longed, this woman had returned to take her away again, back to the ancient cottage where her father had fought out his last agonised days of his sentence of life. Her mother, a rigid white ghost, had gone silently about the home, and a lonely and terrified child had hidden in corners and crept silently away into the bright fantasy world where adult mysteries could never follow.

'And all the time it had been worse for her, because she could not understand.'

Eileen's head was bowed, her eyes closed as the pictures of the first few days passed across her mind. Hardisty reached up and stroked the hair away from her face in a curiously gentle gesture. She started, and looked at him in surprise. He smiled.

'Go on.'

She looked down again.

'When I realised what I'd done to her, I swore I'd never let anything hurt her again.'

A little girl exploring a familiar garden with careful concentration and quiet apprehension. A child walking up the crooked oak stairs, back pressed fearfully against the wall as though a hurrying figure might run down without seeing her; the awful hurt of not being noticed. A little face looking round the door. Can I come in now? The first, uncertain smile.

'She got better quite quickly. Children are very resilient like that. And when they know they can depend on love, nothing else can hold them back.'

Apprehensive tomboy, peering uncertainly through the kitchen door, T-shirt torn, jeans muddy, hairband lost. Does it matter? Tear-streaked face, grazed hands and knees. Please make it better!

'Robin had quite a lot of money. I never realised until he died. It didn't seem to matter. I hadn't had much before then. I was determined Hilary would never go short.'

The determined struggle to understand the terms that the lawyers used; the hours spent in the dusty office of the kindly old stockbroker who had coached her so patiently and advised her so carefully.

'When Hilary was at home I spent all my time with her.'

The long drives in the country, the quick bursts down the motorway. 'Gosh, *that* was fast!' The rides across the moors and the hurt, indignant dismay when the beloved new pony had bucked her off. The picnics in the holidays, the shared plans for future excursions.

'We travelled quite a lot in the summer. We'd take the car over to France, and just head off wherever we liked.'

Cheeks flushed with excitement as the big car roared down the wide German autobahns; furious concentration on the struggle with schoolgirl French to ask directions from a patient and courteously attentive gendarme; shy, stumbling thanks as a beaming Italian shopkeeper pinned a huge flower to her hat and planted a smacking kiss on her cheek.

'I suppose I made Hilary my life.'

Eileen looked down at Hardisty, and smiled uncertainly.

'When you nearly lose a child . . .' she hesitated, and turned her head away. When she spoke again her voice was a whisper, and he barely caught her words.

'She becomes very dear to you.'

CHAPTER THIRTEEN

In view of the apparent severity of his injuries, it seems that Hardisty recovered extremely fast. The woman who lived in the flat opposite Eileen told me she had seen 'the American gentleman' up and about within a week and had asked him how he had hurt himself. He had told her he had fallen off a motor bicycle, a story she had accepted without question.

Relations between Hardisty and Eileen Denham certainly improved during that time. Eileen, having achieved her object, gave up working at the club with a relief that was matched by that of her employers. Hardisty, without making any further attempt to dissuade Eileen from continuing with her scheme, told her a great deal about his home and his life in California. Eileen listened with more than a casual interest. In spite of Walshe's vehement protestations to the contrary, I am inclined to believe that Eileen was considering the prospect of returning to the United States with Hardisty very seriously; she was certainly beginning to believe that the man who had murdered the three children had escaped the consequences of his brutal actions, and the removal of the responsibility she felt had been imposed upon her left her feeling free to take decisions that would irrevocably remove her from the unhappy position in which she had been placed.

Hardisty was certainly very much in love with her. Eileen's horror at the extent of his injuries was obviously not assumed and he accepted without question her explanation that she had asked her friends to delay him for a couple of hours, never imagining that they would use such drastic methods. Her feelings of guilt diminished as he recovered, and it was not long before their relationship was on an easy footing. Eileen began to remember the happy years she had spent with Robin Denham and to wonder whether she might not be equally happy with Dan Hardisty.

Strangely enough, one of the factors that deterred her was the short time that she had known him before he asked her to live with him. This made her wonder whether he did not regard their relationship as being purely transitory and she lacked the confidence in herself to take what she felt was a risk. Hardisty, unaware of these doubts, made the mistake of assuming it was her own lack of feeling for him that was holding her back and felt that he would do better to allow her time to make up her own mind.

He made no attempt to find out where Eileen had hidden the gun and she, at first puzzled by his apparent lack of concern, finally decided that his conviction that the man had got away was responsible. If anything she was relieved and so, when he finally did find the ancient carbine by accident, she bore the loss with apparent fortitude.

Eileen was working in the kitchen at the time and Hardisty, bored with watching her and unable to help because of his bandaged hand, was wandering around the flat looking at her books and pictures while he waited for her to finish. As he walked past the bed he felt the loose floorboard rock under his feet. He stopped, stepped back and tested it again. He bent down and pulled back the rug, examining the board.

'Eileen, do you have a hammer?'

'Just a minute.'

Hardisty squatted down and levered the board out of place. He looked down into the cavity, and a slight smile crossed his face as he saw the gun. He lifted it out, the smile fading as he noticed the worn and pitted barrel and felt the play in the receiver. Shaking his head in disgust, he took the gun by the barrel, raised it over his head and smashed it down on to the floor.

Eileen, hearing the crash, ran in from the kitchen. Hardisty looked up and grinned at her horrified expression.

'I don't know about your target,' he said, 'but I doubt if you'd have survived using that.'

Eileen walked across the room and sat on the bed. 'Oh, bloody hell!'

Hardisty stood up, looked at the gun to ensure that it was completely smashed, and kicked it to one side.

'You've got a perfectly good rifle back in Hallerton,' he said. 'Why don't you wait until you can use that?'

'Two hundred quid that cost me,' said Eileen in disgust. 'Two hundred bloody quid, and you've smashed it.'

'You were robbed.'

'I know that. Damned vandal. Why don't you mind your own business?'

He reached over and ruffled her hair. 'Terrible, isn't it? Wilful destruction of property. How about that? Nothing worse than a crooked copper, is there?'

Eileen choked back a laugh. He sat down beside her.

'And the trouble you went to getting it,' he mused.

'Rat.'

'And hiding it. And stopping me following you.'

'Bastard.'

'And what do I do?' He shook his head sadly. 'I drop it. Didn't realise it was so fragile.'

Eileen scowled at him, and he laughed.

'Never mind, honey. I'll buy you another one. One like mine.'

'What's that?'

'Winchester.'

'Give me back my own Lee Enfield, you damned patronising Yank. I don't want your rotten American pea-shooters.'

'Okay.' He lay back on the bed, his hands behind his head. 'We'll go hunting together,' he said. 'Ever been on a hunting trip? No, of course you haven't. Maybe we could take Terry. Camp out somewhere. Would you like that?'

She was smiling faintly, her chin cupped in her hands. He opened one eye and surveyed her thoughtfully.

'How about it?' he asked.

'I don't like killing things.'

'No? Funny, that wasn't the impression you gave me. Maybe it's a bit of a come-down. Rabbits after the big game you were planning on.'

'Rabbits? I thought it was other hunters you shot over there.'

'Need a special permit for that.'

Eileen turned and looked at him. 'You know, you really baffle me. I say all these awful things about America and you never get annoyed. Why not?'

'Self control.' He reached out a hand and pulled her down beside him, rolling towards her and burying his face in her hair. 'Lots of self control. Let me show you what I mean.'

'Hmm?'

'Get those clothes off.'

'Let me go. You'll open those cuts again.' She made a half-hearted effort to push him away, and he laughed.

'Damn right. Keep your teeth and nails to yourself this time.'

Eileen stopped struggling, and looked up at him with a smile. 'Do I chew you up?'

'Yeah. You're a cannibal.'

'Do you mind?'

'You talk too much, that I mind. Nothing else.'

'Can you tell me how you found out about the gun?' I asked Walshe.

'The second one?'

'Yes.'

'Searched her flat. You know. Routine thing to do. Floorboard was still loose. There it was. Smashed up.'

'What sort of gun was it?'

'Rifle. Old one. Dreadful thing, downright dangerous. Ballistics fella nearly had a fit when he saw it. Rotten with rust. Woodworm in the stock.'

'Did she have any ammunition?'

'Not for that gun. Had some 7.62 ammunition for the other one. This was a .303.'

'Surely she'd have realised it was the wrong size?'

'You'd think so. Funny, that.' Walshe frowned, and looked across at me. 'Getting me worried, you are. You know. Hadn't thought about that. Suppose I assumed she'd have got some later. Maybe I was wrong. Maybe she was starting to see sense.'

'Could that have made any difference to your case?'

'Not to the facts. But I slated Dan Hardisty in court. Maybe I was a bit unfair.'

He looked away, worried and unhappy, and I found myself attempting to justify his position.

'She hadn't really had time to get any more ammunition though, had she? And there wasn't any point in getting it after the gun was smashed.'

'That's right.' He sounded unconvinced and I changed the subject.

'Did Dan Hardisty get back on time when his leave expired?'

'Yes. Patched up with Elastoplast. Said he'd fallen off a motor bike. Cut himself on glass.'

'Did you believe him?'

'Why not?'

'How much longer was he going to stay on?'

'He got an extra six weeks. Said he might be able to come back if anything happened after that.'

'But the case broke before then?'

'Yes. You know how it happened?'

It happened, as the police were the first to admit, by a stroke of pure luck. Late one night in early March a patrolling policeman, Sergeant Peter Evans, was stopped by a woman whose name had become a byword in the force for nosy interference in other people's business. In conspiratorial tones she informed Sergeant Evans that a window in one of the garages behind her house had blown open, and she had gone to secure it because the noise was disturbing her. She had looked through the window and noticed a pile of pornographic magazines on the floor. She felt it was her duty to report it, and insisted on accompanying Sergeant Evans to the scene.

She must have been disappointed by his reaction. He gave the pile of illegal literature little more than a cursory glance and then turned his attention to the car that the garage also housed, a dark green Vauxhall Viva.

Unwilling to give the inquisitive woman any further food for gossip, he contented himself with making a note of the address of the garage and the registration number of the car, relying on his accurate memory to report the rusted sills, the dented hub caps, and the fact that the tax disc stuck to the dusty windscreen was more than two years out of date. As soon as he was out of earshot he radioed the information back to the police station, and five minutes later a patrol car collected him and took him back to see Chief Superintendent Black.

The following morning a check on the records at the tax office showed that the car listed under that particular number had been reported as scrapped two years before. The owner, Terence Joss, was part owner of a small second-hand car business. Further checks showed that the Vauxhall had apparently been taken in part exchange a week prior to the alleged scrapping of the car, and nothing more had been heard about it.

Walshe, Stewart and Hardisty returned to Hallerton that afternoon: Walshe and Stewart jubilant and confident, and Hardisty surprisingly subdued and thoughtful. On their arrival they had a conference with Chief Superintendent Black. Their main problem was collecting sufficient information to apply for a warrant without arousing their suspect's suspicions. Finally, they decided to apply for the warrant on the grounds of the possession of the pornographic magazines, which appeared to be stacked in bundles ready for re-distribution, and use the powers that would be given them on its strength to complete their investigations into the crime in which they were primarily concerned.

Dick Farley and a young detective constable, John Malloy, carried out the arrest, and Joss' reactions did nothing to lessen their suspicions. At first he denied all knowledge of the garage and then, when Farley pointed out that the lease was in the name of his business, he said that it had nothing to do with him; his partner was responsible and should have terminated the lease three years before.

Back at the police station Farley questioned him further.

Joss demanded that his solicitor should be present, then changed his mind when offered the use of a telephone. Up to that time, Farley had made no mention of the Vauxhall, which was being rigorously searched by a team of policemen, but Joss, becoming more and more agitated, said that he had told a fitter to take the car up to the council tip and he did not know that it was in the garage.

At this point Farley telephoned Walshe, who conducted the rest of the interview. Joss claimed that Farley had told him about the car and said that Farley had threatened to beat him up if he did not admit it was his car. Walshe asked him why he was so anxious about the car, and he refused to reply. Once again, he demanded the right to call his solicitor, and this time he did so. Walshe left until the lawyer arrived.

He already knew that a serrated edged knife and a cassette recorder had been found in the car and was convinced, as were all the men involved, that Joss was the man they had been seeking. While they were waiting for the solicitor he and Stewart checked the questionnaire form that Joss had filled in the previous autumn. Written on the back, and signed by one of the patrolmen who had been involved in the enquiry, were the words 'seemed uncertain of whereabouts at time "A". No substantiation of whereabouts at time "B".' Joss had claimed to have been road testing a car alone at the time that the Butler child was killed, and to have been at home, or at work, when Janice Clayton died. The second questionnaire, filled in after the death of Hilary Denham, stated that he had been at the garage. There were no comments on the back of the form, but again there was no substantiation of his claim. He said that he did not own a cassette recorder and did not know his blood group.

Shortly after Walshe and Stewart finished reading the questionnaires a further interim report came in from the men searching the car and garage. They had not found any spools of tape for the recorder, but samples of cloth fibre and sweepings from the carpet had been sent back to the laboratory. Several fingerprints had been found and it seemed probable that some were those of children. There were no traces of bloodstains, but small flakes in the serrated edge of the knife could be dried blood. The knife, incidentally, was a saw-toothed German bayonet. An army jack knife had also been found and both weapons were on their way to the laboratory for examination.

Walshe asked Black to apply for a search warrant for the second-hand car business premises and Joss' home. He himself went back for a further interview with the suspect.

The solicitor arrived as he was about to enter the little room in which Farley and Joss were waiting. Walshe told him that the charge at present was concerned solely with the possession of pornographic literature, but the solicitor insisted that his client had spoken of unfair questioning designed to implicate him in the recent murder investigation. Joss' words had been 'They're trying to pin those murders on me'. The solicitor, Mr Angier, pointed out that Walshe's presence did seem to lend some credence to Joss' fears and asked for an explanation. Walshe replied that any information on this would be given to him at the proper time, but that no charges were being made at that time.

The second interview was purely a formality. Joss was formally charged and the solicitor, after warning his client to make no statement unless he was present, left.

Later that afternoon the evidence for which they had been waiting arrived. Two fingerprints in the car were those of Hilary Denham, one was matched with Janice Clayton's prints, the stains on the bayonet were human blood and Joss' fingerprints were on the hilt. Hairs found on the upholstery of the passenger seat matched those of Hilary Denham, and the fingerprints on the steering wheel, gear lever and hand brake showed that the car had last been driven by Joss.

'No way of getting round that evidence,' said Walshe. 'Bloody marvellous. Never had so much in my life. We'd got him.'

'Did you ever find the cassette tapes?'

'No. Who needed them? We had more than enough. He hadn't a shred of evidence in defence. Solicitor knew it. Looked pretty gloomy when he heard our case.'

'So your job was just about over?'

He nodded. 'Routine after that. Making out reports. Far as I was concerned it was as good as done. Or so I thought.'

A point that Walshe did not mention, probably imagining that I knew as much, if not more than, he did, was the reaction of the Press.

Following the thorough preliminary search of the car, it was loaded on to a trailer and towed back to the police station by a police Land Rover. It was inevitable that somebody, noticing the Vauxhall, would draw the correct conclusion and notify the Press.

The switchboard at Hallerton police station was inundated with calls from enquiring reporters. The operators, obeying instructions, attempted to play the matter down. Black, furious with the unfortunate policeman who had neglected to put a tarpaulin over the car before displaying it to enquiring eyes, gave up the unequal struggle and asked the Press not to publish until the committal proceedings were over.

His cautious attitude was entirely justified. Previous similar cases had shown that public reaction could be extremely violent, and he was motivated by fears for the safety of his prisoner should news of the arrest come out prematurely. He

179

remembered a case when a mob of furious women had attacked a police vehicle containing a suspected child murderer, hammering on it and screaming for the man to be handed over to them and he had no intention of allowing a similar incident to occur in this case. Public feeling was still very high.

The Press were, on the whole, remarkably co-operative. Some national papers announced that Walshe, Stewart and Hardisty were back in the Midlands, but the few enquiries that this brought were easily dealt with; the case was not closed and would not be until the murderer was caught. The three men were simply checking on progress. They would certainly be returning from time to time.

I was in London at the time and had been in the offices of my paper when the telephone call from Hallerton came through, asking for our co-operation and promising interviews and details of the case after the committal proceedings. There was, not unnaturally, a considerable stir of interest, and a hasty conference was held at which it was decided to send a reporter and a photographer up to Hallerton to keep an eye on things, and to keep a careful ear to the ground in case any other newspaper decided to publish. The newspaper, while prepared to offer all possible assistance to the police, was not going to allow rivals less scrupulous to steal the cream off one of the biggest stories of the decade and we were all on the alert for any hint that one of them was preparing to do so.

Diane Clayton came into my office early that afternoon with some photographs for an article I was writing. I was not aware that a photographer had already been chosen and so, as I was glancing through the photographs, I asked a casual question.

'Do you know Hallerton?'

I was looking closely at one of the photographs at the time, so I did not see the expression on her face. After a moment she replied.

'Yes, slightly. Why?'

'It looks as if they've got the child killer. We got word this morning.'

'Do they want me to go up and cover it?'

I put down the photographs and looked up. 'I don't think so. It isn't up to me anyway. We're not printing anything about it just yet. They want the committal proceedings over first.'

'When will that be?'

'Thursday morning in Hallerton. After that we can go to town.'

Diane asked nothing more. I chose a couple of photographs, we exchanged a few commonplaces, and she left.

I did not see her again for over a year.

Diane returned to her flat immediately she left my office and telephoned Eileen. It never became entirely clear what was said at the time, but it seems probable that Diane, on hearing that Eileen had not got a gun, had herself formulated the plan whereby Eileen would return to Brighton, visit Jackie Grey on what seemed to be a social call, take his keys and have them copied, return later in the day to collect a pair of gloves and replace the keys before they were missed.

The gunsmith later said that Eileen appeared to be in a dazed condition when she called on him and it seems most unlikely that she would have been capable of working out such a plan, simple though it was.

Eileen returned to the shop late that night and took a gun almost identical to the one she had purchased the previous autumn. The bolts of the rifles were kept in a secure cupboard in the workshop, and Eileen was perhaps unlucky in that she took a bolt that Jackie had been working on the day before; had she not done so he might not have missed the gun for several days. As it was, he noticed that the bolt was missing the following morning, and a quick search disclosed that the rifle had also gone.

He telephoned the police, who called round later in the morning. He did not associate the missing gun with Eileen's visit and was baffled as to how an intruder had managed to enter his premises. The police took details of the gun and left after a brief check around. The matter of the missing rifle was not treated lightly, but it seemed improbable that the case would be solved.

'Tuesday, that was,' said Walshe in answer to my question. 'She went back to London. Stayed with the Clayton woman, drove up to Hallerton early on the Thursday. Got up on the roof of those flats overlooking the court house. You know the ones? We'd checked them of course. Routine thing to do. One of the coppers who went there said he'd told the caretaker not to let anybody up there. Caretaker denied it. Take your pick. She got there after they'd left. Said she wanted to take photographs for postcards and slipped him a fiver. Good view of the area from there. There she was. View straight into the car park.'

'A good place for a shot?'

'Christ, no. Wouldn't say that. Difficult angle, downwards like that. Looks easy on the films. Not so good in practice.'

'Wouldn't she have known that?'

He shook his head. 'Probably not. Only ever shot on a range. Wouldn't know much about practical problems like that.'

'When did Dan Hardisty find out she was there?'

Walshe looked at me in silence. At last he shrugged. 'I was pretty busy that morning. Didn't know what Dan was doing. Didn't see him. Only found out later, when it was all over.'

From the time that the three men had gone back to Hallerton, Hardisty had tried constantly to contact Eileen Denham. He did not know if she was aware of recent events and, had it not been for the fact that she had somehow learned of the chase following the hit and run incident, he might have gambled on her having heard nothing of the arrest and impending committal hearings. Had he been free to do so, he would probably have gone to Glasgow and stayed with her until the entire trial had been completed. As it was, he could not leave Hallerton without telling Walshe everything that had happened, a course that would have resulted in the inevitable termination of his own career and a very bleak outlook indeed for Eileen.

The dilemma, as his defence counsel later pointed out, must have been appalling.

As Thursday approached he grew more and more frantic. There was no reply to the telephone at her flat in Glasgow and the one in Brighton had been disconnected. In desperation, he tried to persuade Walshe that she should appear for the prosecution at the committal proceedings, which would have enabled him to use official means to find her, but Walshe could see no necessity for that; he was not even sure whether she would be called at the Assizes.

Hardisty telephoned Brighton C.I.D. and asked them to call on Eileen at the Brighton address. He gave some minor excuse for his request, but was not surprised when they called back later that day to say she had left the flat some months earlier and had apparently not returned.

In fact, he did everything he could to trace her, and by the time the Thursday of the committal proceedings dawned he had exhausted every avenue open to him without result.

CHAPTER FOURTEEN

In spite of the fact that there had been no publicity about the arrest and impending committal proceedings, the security precautions were very strict indeed. They were not, however, based on the possibility of a planned attack; the police fears were of the news of the arrest leaking out, and of an angry crowd gathering at the court, a problem that had arisen in previous similar cases.

The Press were, of course, to be allowed in court. It was not expected that many members of the public would be there and it was hoped that, by the time the enormous number of police around the court was noticed, the brief proceedings would be over and Joss would be safely back in the prison. Anybody other than the Press or lawyers going into the court would be searched.

Parking had been banned in the streets outside and the court was to be surrounded by police from a few minutes before Joss was due to arrive until he had left. There were to be men posted all around the railings surrounding the car park and cars patrolled the area ceaselessly. The men were told to prevent any groups of people forming in the area.

Nobody thought it necessary to issue them with arms.

If Hardisty was reassured by these precautions, it was not noticeable in his demeanour. He was short-tempered and irritable, constantly checking details and raising objections. A humorous quip from Palmer about differing attitudes on the other side of the Atlantic was met with a blistering retort and a suggestion that the startled sergeant return to catching shoplifters and mind his own goddamned business. Hardisty now was a very different man from the equable and pleasant character who had first come to Hallerton a year before. If Walshe noticed the difference he made no mention of it, but the men with whom Hardisty was working were puzzled and resentful. They became less and less inclined to listen to his objections and suggestions and he, unable to tell them of what he feared, found their unhelpful attitude maddening.

It was perhaps because of his frustrated exasperation that he took his gun with him when he set off for the police station on the Thursday morning. He was fully aware that no arms were to be issued, that his action was an intolerable departure from normal and permitted procedure and it is unlikely that he gave any consideration at all to the implications behind that hasty decision. It is impossible to say whether at that time he had considered using the gun as a last, desperate resort.

Black, having noticed Hardisty's extreme preoccupation with the security arrangements, had offered to put him in charge of checking them during the time the committal proceedings were in progress, an offer which Hardisty had accepted with alacrity. He arrived at the court early and ran quickly, almost perfunctorily, through the routine that was to be followed there. Eileen's attack, if it came at all, would take place outside.

Joss was to be driven to the rear entrance of the court and taken from the van through a door that led directly into the car park. This door was at the top of a flight of steps, and the van was to draw up a few yards away from these steps. The danger, as Hardisty saw it, would be at its height during the times that Joss was between the van and the building on his arrival and his departure.

Hardisty stood at the top of the flight of steps and scanned the surrounding area intently.

The police station backed on to the far end of the car park. On one side there was a school playing-field, deserted apart from two uniformed policemen pacing slowly along the railings. Hardisty glanced at them cursorily and turned to look at the road on the other side where people were already walking on their way to work.

He did not raise his eyes to the blocks of flats that towered over the shops and houses on that street.

Joss was due to arrive at eleven that morning. At a quarter to eleven the security arrangements were put into effect. Policemen lined the railings of the car park, stood on the steps of the court and searched people coming in. Hardisty walked from one group to the next, warning them yet again to look out for cars stopping near the railings, for people loitering near the court and, almost as an afterthought, for groups of people forming nearby. They listened impassively, nodding, and raised their eyebrows at each other as he walked away.

At eleven o'clock precisely the dark blue van with the barred windows turned down the slope into the car park, still preceded by two motor cycle outriders, and pulled to a halt at the foot of the steps.

Hardisty, standing in the centre of the car park, scanned the road quickly, glanced at the group of men hurrying the handcuffed figure up the steps, looked again at the road and the entrance to the car park, then turned back to the concrete building as the door slammed shut. He released his pent up breath in a long sigh, feeling his heart thudding against his ribs. Slowly, he walked back to the court house.

Eileen lowered the rifle slowly, her face blank with incomprehension. It had happened too fast. She had not been ready, had not had time to pull the trigger. She had not realised they would be so quick.

She closed her eyes and leaned against the low parapet, struggling to bring herself back under control.

She had to get him when he came out. She must get ready now.

Wearily, she turned and looked down towards the car park again, raised the gun and rested the barrel on the wall.

The cross hairs of the sight were lined on the green paint of the door. Patiently, she waited for that door to open. This time, she must do it.

The committal proceedings were brief and formal. Walshe gave a quick résumé of the evidence for the prosecution. Joss was remanded in custody.

At a signal from a policeman at the entrance to the car park the driver of the van started the engine. Hardisty drew in his breath as he heard it revving and looked around the car park again. He glanced up as the green door swung open, then turned back to look along the road, at the policemen who stood along the railings.

When he looked back at the flight of steps, the group of men were still standing outside the door, Joss in their midst. He felt a surge of anger.

'*Get him into that bloody van!*'

Farley raised a hand in acknowledgement, and stepped forward.

The first bullet ploughed through the wood of the door and shattered the brick behind it, raising a cloud of dust and rubble.

For Hardisty, everything leapt into place with startling clarity. He spun round and stared up at the tall buildings from where the shot had come.

'Christ Almighty!' Farley was yelling. 'Get him back inside!'

The second shot hit the handrail beside the flight of steps, the metal buckling under the impact.

'*No*, Eileen,' said Hardisty aloud. 'Don't do it. Don't shoot again.'

He saw the men at the railings staring down in amazement. The next shot would hit somebody. Almost as though he were standing beside her, he could see Eileen raising the rifle again, her finger tightening on the trigger.

When he turned back to the group on the steps his gun was in his hand. He raised it, aimed and fired.

Joss was dead before he hit the ground.

At last Walshe sighed and looked up at me. 'Tore his bloody throat out,' he said simply. 'Nearly blasted his head off.'

I nodded, and said nothing.

'Powerful guns, those things,' he mused. 'He was a good shot too.'

'He got life, didn't he?'

'Oh, yes. What else?'

'What happened to Eileen Denham?'

He shook his head sadly. 'Poor woman. She was finished. Found her walking along the road carrying that rifle. When we picked her up she didn't know what was going on. Just kept saying "Hilary, Hilary" over and over again. Shouldn't think she'll ever recover now.'

He stared down at his clasped hands, and sighed again. 'What a bloody shambles.'

I finally saw Dan Hardisty about two months later. I had written to him asking if he would be willing to see me and explaining what I was trying to do. He did not reply, but a visiting permit arrived, so I drove down to the prison one Sunday afternoon, hoping to learn something that would give some meaning to the futile tragedy.

He was very thin by then, almost gaunt, his eyes sunken and his cheeks hollow. He greeted me politely, accepted a cigarette and waited for me to start my questions.

I looked around. There were other prisoners seated around similar tables talking to their visitors, smoking and laughing. A child ran up and down the spaces between the tables. An impassive warder stood a few yards away, his arms folded.

When I looked back at Hardisty he had leaned his elbows on the table and cupped his chin in his hands. He smiled as I met his eyes.

'Thank you for agreeing to see me,' I said.

He smiled again, but made no reply.

Suddenly it was very difficult to ask questions. What could I say that would not be trite or impertinent? I drew a deep breath.

'Why did you shoot Joss?'

His expression did not change. It was almost as though he had not heard me. I was about to ask something else when he began to speak.

'If Eileen had shot him she would have gone mad. I knew what sort of a state she'd be in. I'd seen it before. That would have finished her. She'd never have got over it.'

'Do you think she will now?'

He reached out a hand and flicked his cigarette ash into the ashtray.

'No,' he said quietly.

I shivered at the finality in his voice. He noticed the movement and the corners of his mouth lifted again. I could not smile back.

'Did you gain anything at all then?'

'Doesn't seem like it.'

'Do you keep in touch with her?'

'I write. She doesn't reply.'

I looked away. The warder shifted his position, and leaned back against the wall.

'What will you do when you're free again?'

'Bum around,' he said lightly.

'Will you see Eileen again?'

He smiled that same bitter smile again. I wished I had not asked.

'Maybe.'

'Will you go back to the States?'

'Haven't thought yet.'

I felt defeated. I could learn nothing through this barrier of impassivity and I was unwilling to probe too deeply.

We spent the rest of the visit in almost complete silence. He replied to my comments, always with that tight smile on his face, but volunteered nothing himself. I was relieved when the warder, after a look at his wrist watch, called out that it was time to finish the visit.

He stood up and thanked me for coming to see him. I said something in reply, and he turned away.

'Good luck with your book,' he said politely.

'Thank you.'

I watched the prisoners file out of the room. Hardisty did not look back.

The door closed behind them.